Bassin' Assassin

Everett Melnick

VANTAGE PRESS
New York

For Linda Thompson

FIRST EDITION

Published by Vantage Press, Inc.
516 West 34th Street, New York, New York 10001

Manufactured in the United States of America
ISBN: 0-533-13776-4

Library of Congress Catalog Card No.: 00-093258

0 9 8 7 6 5 4 3 2 1

Bassin' Assassin

Prologue

Give a man a fish and he eats for a day; teach a man to fish and he eats for life read the inscription on a plastic plate on the lid of a fishing tackle box. Above the inscription was the name *Sam Allen*. Brad stared at it for a few minutes, fought back tears, and with a lump in his throat, slowly opened the top. *You can tell a lot about a person from his tackle box,* Brad thought to himself. He smiled in recognition as he looked at the order in which the lures were arranged. It was obvious his father had been a very organized man. Each hook, weight, and lure was in its own small compartment, in its own tray. Brad presumed this was an example of his father's inflexible personality.

The majority of baits were large. Brad remembered his father saying, "Big baits catch big fish." Brad thought this merely illustrated how resolute his father was, as he remembered how hard he pulled on his rod to set the hook.

"You've got to cross their eyes," he'd say, when he admonished his son for losing a fish.

In the largest compartment in the bottom of the box were the soft plastic baits, by far his father's favorites. Brad saw this as an indication of his father's gentleness and understanding As any fisherman knows, it takes patience and finesse to work slow moving plastic worms and lizards successfully. He remembered his father spending what seemed like hours, moving only a few yards, casting accurately at a clump of bushes here, or a partially submerged stump there. Sometimes, convinced that a fish was in residence, he'd repeatedly cast to the same spot, three, four or five times, clenching his jaw in a self-satisfied grin, when the line finally jumped or slowly moved off. He would set the hook, giving Brad the look he knew so well, which meant there was a lesson to be learned.

1

Brad hated funerals. He'd always hated funerals. Unlike some of his relatives who enjoyed going to them to see how much weight their cousins gained since the last time they had seen them—most likely at another funeral. Sitting in the back seat of the limo, he reached into his jacket pocket and felt about to determine what was left from the last time he had worn this suit. It was kind of a game he played with his dress clothes, because he wore them so infrequently. It was also a way in which he vented some of his nervous energy when he was forced into a situation in which he felt uncomfortable.

A soft gummy object came out with his hand. He didn't recognize it at first by feel. Looking down, he saw a watermelon-colored, soft plastic lizard. Although he was pretty sure he had never worn his black suit fishing, he felt that the lizard belonged there. It was a comfort to him, yet he hesitated to call it a security lizard. It had begun years ago, when he had inadvertently left one in his jacket pocket after a fishing trip. The occasion had not presented itself for him to dispose of it without causing mild hysteria amongst his companions at the time. That in itself gave him pause to be nervous. Somehow rolling it between his fingers had a tranquilizing effect.

The limousine pulled away from the curb and headed down familiar streets to the front door of an all too familiar funeral parlor. The driver opened the door for him but he hesitated, figuring the longer he took, the less time he'd have to spend inside. Funeral homes, he thought, were supposed to comfort the bereaved, but every time he'd gone to one, someone he'd cared about had died. He didn't like the smell of the place. He didn't like the music that drifted through the room even though he'd chosen his father's favorite. It was too dark. It was too warm. The flowers were poorly arranged. The chairs were not very comfortable. He just stood there and stared. The figure in the casket didn't look like his father, at least not like Brad remembered him, but he had to acknowledge that for the first time in a long time, his father looked relaxed and happy. A warm feeling came over him and he felt like saying something very emotional, but knowing it was too late for his father to hear, he reached over and took hold of a lifeless hand, placed his plastic lizard in it, gently laid the hand down, then turned and walked out. It wasn't a gesture of defiance or even disrespect as it might have looked to some who did not know him well. It was Brad's way of expressing his grief and he didn't feel he had to apologize or explain to anyone.

Fishing was not Brad's whole life, but it was certainly the only part he liked to be awake for. His father had put a fishing pole in his hands when he was three. It wasn't a "snoopy" outfit, it was a real fiberglass rod with a genuine bait casting reel wound with black cotton fishing line. Backlashes and snags were left to him to deal with. It taught him patience as well as a few bad words. Brad's father had been heard to say of his son, "If breathing wasn't automatic, he'd be found dead with a rod and reel in his hand and with any luck, a largemouth bass on the end of the line."

Brad bought a T-shirt once that read "Fishing is life, the rest is just details." Those details, he now reflected, made him somewhat of a disappointment to his father, whose desire to see his son become an engineer was always at odds with Brad's love of fishing. He tried engineering, but after two years at college he knew more about the bottom contours of the local reservoir than calculus, physics or chemistry.

During vacations, while fishing with his father, Brad tried to convince him that he would be better served quitting school and trying his hand at guiding, with hopes of following the pro fishing circuit. Sam Allen told his son if he came home without a college degree, he would change the locks on the doors and Brad would not get a key. The problem was, as much as he took after his father, Brad had not gone through World War I, World War II and the Great Depression, and was not as tough as his father, as Sam Allen had pointed out on several occasions. His mother had tried to help by wringing her hands and crying.

Finally, after six years of changing majors, and having a little knowledge in a lot of areas but no degree, he called it quits. Not that he was wasting his parents' money; he had worked the summers and vacation periods on whatever job paid the most money. He also tried to find jobs in which he could learn something useful. Of course, it never hurt if it turned out that the job was close to a lake or pond where fish were known to be in residence. During the school year, he went out for football and wrestling. Not being enlightened, the schools didn't offer competitive fishing.

For relaxation that didn't involve a hangover, he learned *tai chi*, which gave some purpose and direction to his otherwise ruggedly handsome six-foot-plus, one hundred and ninety pound frame. He found he could handle himself quite well in threatening situations. When the spirit moved him to raise his hand against someone, they usually were the worse for it.

The girls could lose themselves in his deep blue eyes, but he simply thought they reflected the waters he'd just as soon be fishing on. A mirror held no comfort for him as he kept trying to see his father's reflection looking back at him, but saw only a part of the man that he hoped to be.

Brad sat his parents down, and told them he had put up with his father trying to relive his own life through him long enough, and had decided to live his own life from this point on. If necessary, he was prepared to go his own way.

His father said to no one in particular, "This is how we get repaid for all our years of sacrifice." His mother sniffed back a tear.

After twenty-five years, including six years at college, he had not mastered Guilt 101. He begged for their forgiveness and understanding during this difficult time in his life, and promised to repay them for all of their sacrifices.

Within a year, his mother was diagnosed with, treated for, and died from cancer. Though never blamed, references were made to the correlation between the disease and severe stress. Here, Brad started on a guilt trip he had never ended, and wasn't sure he ever would. As tough a front as he put up, Brad's father could not face life without her. Brad had little doubt that his mother's stoic support helped make his father the rugged individual he perceived himself to be.

Shortly after the funeral, Brad came home from work one day to find his father sitting in his chair, staring off into space. Asking him if he was okay, his father replied, "Your mother was here today. She followed me around the house. I tried to talk to her . . . I think I'm losing my mind." Brad led his father to his bedroom, helped him to undress and get into bed like a helpless child. He passed away quietly in his sleep. From the look on his father's face when he found him in the morning, Brad was sure that his father and mother were together once again.

The funeral was now only a blur. It was hard for him to mourn as he was sure his father was happier in death than he could ever have been living alone. Brad found it hard to picture either of his parents alone. It had always been the two of them. In fact, as he reflected back over the years, he couldn't remember a time they were apart. Their personalities, different as they were, always seemed to complement each other. He began to believe that one could not possibly exist without the other. He felt happy then. He no longer thought of them as sick or lonely or even old. Rather, he saw his father standing on some forgotten shore, a casting rod in his hands, his mother sitting in a lawn chair by his side, getting some sun or writing a letter to a friend or relative. It mattered not that they were dressed in polyester, for it could have been yesterday.

"Brad? Brad, could I speak to you for a minute?"

It was Uncle George, his father's brother from some little town in Texas near the Louisiana border. His father had told him that he had moved down there twenty or so years ago to go into the boat building business. It seemed the temperature and humidity were just about perfect for working with resins, the stuff used to make fiberglass boats.

Other than the Stetson hat and cowboy boots, he looked exactly as he had the last time Brad had seen him, five or ten years ago. If you had put Uncle George next to his brother, no one would ever think them related. Sam Allen, being the eldest, favored his mother: tall, slim and well-built, his posture and demeanor belied his age.

Uncle George, on the other hand, took after Brad's grandfather: he was short, stocky, nearly bald but sharing the same gene pool. Beneath his rather frumpy exterior was the same strength, coordination and resolve that he shared with his brother. Outwardly, Sam looked like someone to reckon with while Uncle George looked like a man whose hardest work was moving from the couch to the refrigerator with an occasional side trip to the liquor cabinet. Once Brad said as much to his father, who reminisced that when they were younger, Uncle George may well have been the staunchest of them all. Something to do with being the youngest in the family and having something to prove.

"It's been a long time, Uncle George," Brad said as he stretched out his hand. George's fingers felt kind of prickly, like those of someone who had been handling insulation without gloves.

He must have noticed Brad's reaction, because he pulled his hand back, apologizing profusely. George explained he had been working on a new boat hull model, and that he personally did the fiberglass work on prototypes.

"Brad," he said, "you look just like your father when he was your age. Seems like only yesterday." He trailed off with just a hint of a Southwestern drawl. "It has been a long time. I'm sorry I didn't make it to your mother's funeral, but I was on a business trip, and I wasn't notified until it was too late." George appeared to be concentrating on something else, then he shook himself slightly and continued. "I don't work out in the factory myself much anymore, I just putter around on a few experimental models with materials like carbon and graphite fiber and fiberglass composites. I like to lay the material by hand, just to be sure that if a hull fails, it's a design flaw and not a manufacturing problem."

Brad was fascinated that all of this information was coming from the man who, twenty years earlier, Sam Allen had said "didn't know a bass boat from a bucket."

"Brad, I've been following your progress for several years now," George said. "Your father called me a while back and told me that you were really something. He said you were smarter than he could ever hope to be, and with your schooling and practical experience, you could do anything you put your hand to and make a success of it. He was very proud of you, but you know it wasn't his style to tell you so."

Brad's eyes welled up with tears, and strangely, he thought of his plastic lizard.

"What are you going to do now?" Uncle George asked tentatively.

"I haven't given it much thought," Brad answered with a curious look.

"Still fishing?" he rejoined.

"Yes, I . . . look, I don't mean any disrespect, but you've obviously got something on your mind."

George laughed. It was a laugh that Brad remembered: sort of an asthmatic chuckle.

"Your father, rest his soul, was sure right. You catch on real quick. Listen, son, this isn't exactly the time and place to talk business, but how about coming back home with me to Texas? My company is sponsoring a bass tournament next weekend. You and I can be fishing partners. We'll have a couple of days to pre-fish and get to know each other. Then we can talk about business and your future."

Brad hadn't planned on going anywhere. He didn't feel like doing anything. In fact, he had never really planned anything in his entire life. He just existed from day to day, mostly doing what other people told him to do, partly from force of habit and partly from guilt. He probably could have been diagnosed as clinically depressed if he had bothered to go to a doctor, but another family trait he tried to live down was a slight tendency toward hypochondria. A fishing tournament, now that just might be the thing to remedy his troubles—an opportunity to talk about the good times and the bad, without the hurt and depression that seemed to be his constant companion. He felt he needed time and space to sort things out. His life and everything he held dear was a shambles. Too many things had happened over which he had no control, and he didn't like that feeling. It was the same reason he never drank much in college or tried the drug scene. Perhaps this was what it felt like to be really grown up and mature. He wasn't sure he liked it, but a bass fishing tournament on Toledo Bend Reservoir, on the Texas-Louisiana border, now that was something. Something Brad felt he needed.

He barely remembered the ride to the cemetery. He stood at the right times and kneeled at the right times. The words he repeated seemed to hold no meaning. His farewells were said a long time ago. Small segments of his life, mainly those of some significance which involved his parents, good and bad, filled his mind. It was like one of those old nickelodeon machines where the still pictures flutter past, giving the appearance of motion.

And then it was over. The last aunt kissed him, her heavy perfume spoiling the fragrance of the wet grass and the newly dug earth. The last cousin shook his hand and patted him on the back. It had rained gently throughout the afternoon and his hands were damp and his back was wet.

The limo driver opened the door and stepped aside so

Brad could get out. The rain had stopped and patches of sun were beginning to peek through the gaps in the clouds. Brad stood for several minutes, looking at his house without recognition. It was the only home he had known for all but the last six school years of his life. Yet now, it was like seeing it for the very first time. Without his parents, it was empty and cold. It had no soul, no spirit, no life. Only memories.

He had some things to take care of, part of his life to put on hold. His Uncle George made the arrangements for them to get to Hemphill, Texas. They were to take a flight to Shreveport, Louisiana, where Uncle George's car was at the airport. From there, it was about a two-hour drive to his house.

At this time of year, the weather on the Texas-Louisiana border was anybody's guess: warm and balmy, or maybe cold and rainy with high winds and thunderstorms. Moisture and warm air from the Gulf, cold air from the north, and winds from the west could make for great fishing, good fishing or no fishing. So while they waited for the plane to take off, Brad gathered his wits together and thought about what he knew about Toledo Bend.

He had read enough to know it was a mainstream reservoir covering approximately 186,000 acres, which were impounded by damming the Sabine River, the natural boundary between Texas and Louisiana. He remembered his father's story about how the Army Corps of Engineers anticipated it taking three years for the reservoir to fill. During that time, local contractors were to harvest the pine, cedar and oak trees, covering the area which would soon be underwater. However, because of the unpredictable weather patterns, torrential rains filled the reservoir, not in three years, but in only one.

Thousands of acres of timber were left flooded by as much as sixty feet of water, perfect structures for bass. Over the years, much of the flooded timber rotted away and had been replaced by aquatic vegetation as bass habitat, some of it on vast shallow grass flats. Still, dense stands of submerged timber made it extremely difficult to get around by boat, unless one knew and followed the boat lanes, which were old road beds or creek and river channels. Most professional bass fisherman would rate Toledo Bend Reservoir among the ten best bass fishing lakes in the country.

The Bend, as locals call it, is nearly eighty miles long and four miles wide at Pendelton Bridge, its narrowest point. In the early days after the lake was formed, many resorts and marinas were built expecting to attract recreational boaters as well as fishermen. Because of its location and extremely challenging conditions, the anticipated crowds never transpired. As a result, many had fallen into disrepair or had been totally abandoned.

Brad's father who had been to Toledo Bend only once, commented on the economically depressed condition of the cities and small towns in the surrounding area. He said jobs were scarce and welfare was becoming a way of life. People who did work were employed in lumbering, supplying logs for the "'creosote" operations scattered throughout the area. Some small oil and gas well fields dotted the area and provided a few job opportunities. Little wonder George Allen chose this place to build a boat factory, the right climate, cheap property, cheap labor and a stone's throw from one of the most challenging sport fisheries in the United States.

The flight was scheduled to last about two hours, which Brad thought would give him time to find out the real reason why his uncle, whom he hadn't seen in years, would suddenly invite him to fish a tournament a thousand miles away. His thoughts ranged from being overly suspicious on the one hand to guardedly grateful on the other. This was not helping to ease his unsettled mind, but he tried to force himself to be cheerfully optimistic.

The plane took off on time, and before he could feel the buzz from his first glass of wine, he was cruising at 35,000 feet.

He had started drinking wine while in college. Unlike most of his acquaintances, Brad had practically no experience with alcohol prior to going away to college. He had tried beer and whiskey drinks but didn't like the speed in which they inebriated him. He found he could sip on a variety of pleasant-tasting wines for hours and not get intoxicated. While his friends drank beer or hard liquor at the same rate, and usually ended up in various degrees of drunkenness, suffering proportionally. He found, probably due to his size and general appearance, that he didn't take much ribbing about his choice of drinks. Further, the slight buzz took the edge off, which at this point, he felt was partly for medicinal purposes. He looked at Uncle George and wondered how he could manage to look as comfortable in the tiny airplane seat, as if he were sitting in his living room in a La-Z-Boy.

George Allen was just about to take a long draw on his first beer when Brad asked, "Why me?"

"Son," he said, without giving the appearance of hearing the question, "something strange is going on at the factory. It started about a month ago. At first, it was little things like doors or windows left open or unlocked. Then, certain items would turn up in places where I was sure they had not been before. Only last week, my computer was left on, when I knew I'd shut the blamed thing off. Have you ever heard of industrial espionage? The boat business is highly competitive, you know. You've got fifteen or twenty small independent boat manufacturers, like me, all trying for a share of the market. If we're successful, a larger corporation is right on our doorstep trying to buy us out.

"None of the companies build a bad boat or they'd be out of business. It's a lot like the automotive industry: the options, graphics, creature comforts and horsepower sell the boats. We're what you'd call a small emerging company. We build about fifteen boats a month, all pretty much by hand. We stress quality and workmanship, not quantity. We're starting to get a good reputation and we sell every boat we build. In fact, we have orders for nearly the next two years in advance! I've been contacted by more than one large conglomerate interested in buying me out, but I run my business carefully, I don't get into the kind of financial problems that have made other small outfits go to the big boys for help.

"In this business, you can come to work one day, and someone else is sitting in your chair, only it isn't yours any longer. That's not going to happen to me, or my boat company. I'm experimenting with a couple of new composite hulls with some pretty exotic new materials and our own process, but it's not top secret, not around here. Other boat companies do the same kinds of things. Hell, some of them do it better than us. I've been very lucky, several pros use our boats, not because I sponsor them, but because they think we have a good product. I've racked my brain trying to figure out what we have that another company would try to steal. Shoot, if they walked up to the front door and asked to come in and look around, I'd probably let them."

He was rambling. Brad could sense that his uncle was trying to sort all of the facts as he knew them, trying to piece them together. He could have been talking to himself.

"How do you know you're not just being paranoid?" Brad asked. The minute the words came out of his mouth, he wished he hadn't said them. He expected his Uncle George to be hurt, to sulk, or even to give him the silent treatment. None of those would have surprised him. His response did.

"You had to ask that, I suppose. Hell, I would have asked that. Come to think of it, I've asked myself that question several times."

"Speaking of questions that have to be asked, what makes you think I can be of any help? First of all, I know practically nothing about building boats. Secondly, I'm not a policeman or detective. Thirdly, I'm not much more than a kid. Fourthly, I never graduated college, and . . . and . . ."

"Please," Uncle George broke in, "listen to what I have to say first, then if you still don't think you can help, or choose not to, just enjoy the fishing tournament and my hospitality. You are really selling yourself short. I happen to know you've had manufacturing experience from your summer work. The engineering courses you took in college, even though you didn't get your degree, should enable you to understand what we're trying to do. I know you've had some classes in law enforcement and criminology, which should give you some insight into anything going on that's not on the up and up. And finally, your father used to complain about all of the art, music and, as he used to say, advanced basket weaving classes that you took. He didn't understand that those classes give depth to your personality, make you a more interesting person, a quality that's difficult to put into words. You can relate to different types of people with diverse interests and personalities, different backgrounds. You're a people person, a difficult commodity to find today, especially with all of your other assets. You're easy to talk to, you actually listen to what other people say, and you're a pretty likable guy."

"You forgot 'walks on water, doesn't get feet wet,'" Brad added sarcastically. "Seriously, how are you going to explain my appearance to the other employees?"

Uncle George gestured to the flight attendant that he needed another beer. Taking his time, he carefully cleaned the pull tab, then opened the can and took a long drink, declaring his satisfaction with a slightly rude sound. He closed his eyes and gathered his thoughts for what seemed like an uncomfortably long time, then held his hands out in a position that might have looked like he was going to pray.

"Look, son, the boat business is all I've got. I put my whole life into it. Your aunt couldn't even take the competition. She often said that she could have put up with another woman, or a bad habit, but she just gave up trying to share me with the boat business. Some women would be proud to have a husband who was trying to build something good. After all, it was for both of us. Maybe if I had put her to work in the business with me, things might have turned out differently.

"She used to rant about having to travel a hundred miles to find a McDonald's. That was her measure of civilization. She didn't make many friends, and she looked down on the locals. I imagine she was mighty lonely. I haven't seen or heard from her in a long time. It's not that I miss her as much as I miss not having had any children. A man builds a business, he'd like to see his own take it over when he decides to take life a little easier. As for explaining you, you're kin. My employees know I have no one to take over from me. They're a bunch of good ol' boys, and most of them have been with me from the start. They believe in what I'm trying to do and they take pride in their work, for which I reward them handsomely. But they're not kin. They understand that in this neck of the woods. If I'm any judge of character, you'll get along just fine once they know you're family. Take your time, look around like you're trying to get the hang of things, talk to them, and play it by ear."

They were silent for a long time. Brad's thoughts were racing. Yesterday his life had no direction and practically no meaning or purpose. Over a rather short period, his world had begun to crumble. Not used to making decisions, he was thrust into a situation calling for action, results, answers and decisions. He was at a crossroads: he could try to help his uncle, or he could fish and go back home. But back home to what? He needed to take responsibility; he needed to grow up; he needed to make changes in his life, his parents would like that.

"Please return your seats to the upright position, fasten your seat belts, and turn off all electronic devices. We will be on the ground in approximately ten minutes."

True to the flight attendant's word, ten minutes later they had deplaned and were standing on the airport concourse. Brad followed his uncle to the exit marked "Parking Lot," walking through row after row of parked vehicles, across a walkway and past a sign indicating "Long-Term Parking" and up to the driver's door of a late model pickup truck with the words *Caliente Bass Boats* neatly lettered in gold leaf on its side. Just below the weather strip under the middle of the window, in small letters was the name *George Allen.*

Brad noticed that the rubber strip was torn directly above the door handle and there seemed to be quite a lot of finger prints and smudge marks in that area of an otherwise clean truck. Turning, he saw Uncle George about to push the keyless entry pad on his key fob.

"Stop," Brad screamed.

The surprise caused George to drop the fob with the keys to the ground.

"What the devil," he shot back. "Now who's paranoid?"

"I'm sorry, maybe it's nothing, but I noticed the torn rubber and smudge marks around the door handle as if someone tried to break in."

"Say, you're right! But why would anyone want to break into this truck? I don't keep anything of value in it. I just use it to run around in and pull a boat now and then." George reflected as he peered in the window.

Brad went around to the other side and looked in the passenger window. He wondered why he was reluctant to open the door or let his uncle unlock his. He had a premonition, a strange feeling unlike any he had ever felt before, almost an invisible force preventing him from allowing the door locks to be opened.

"Why indeed? They didn't even bother to take your car phone."

"Car phone? I don't have a car phone," said Uncle George with a puzzled look on his face.

"I suppose you don't have a radar detector or portable CD player either," Brad said as he walked back to the driver's side and with a wave of his hand, motioned Uncle George to step back away from the truck. George turned his head from side to side, indicating the negative.

"Then you probably have no idea what's plugged into the cigarette lighter receptacle," Brad continued. Again George shook his head, his eyes getting bigger and small beads of perspiration beginning to appear on his forehead. At this point, Brad stepped up into the bed of the truck, looking intently at the sliding rear window. Most of the locks generally consisted of a fairly cheap plastic catch that could easily be released by pushing like so. . . . He slid the panes apart and carefully extended his arm in until he could reach the plug, pulling it with only enough force to remove it from the socket. He then began to gather the plug and wire until a small black metal box came to within his grasp. Withdrawing his hand with its contents, he motioned to Uncle George to open the door locks. While he activated the keyless entry, the loud click indicating the locks had indeed opened, Brad, with the screwdriver blade of his pocket knife, carefully removed the cover of the box and examined the interior.

"Is it a bomb?" asked Uncle George.

"It sure looks like it could be one. This stuff that looks like modeling clay is probably some type of plastic explosive, but it's the circuitry that interests me. All computerized vehicles have something called 'parasitic draw.' It's a very small amount of electricity, continuously drawn from the battery to maintain the computer memory and the memory for the radio stations and the clock. The circuitry in this box detects a sudden increase in electrical flow, like energizing the power door locks and . . . boom!"

The device was incredibly simple. It got the power it needed to function from the lighter socket, but once unplugged it was totally harmless.

"Then someone is trying to kill me," George said, his hand shaking as he tried to put the key into the ignition.

"Not necessarily," Brad speculated, rubbing his forehead. "It might have been just a warning."

"What do you mean a warning? If it weren't for you, someone would be trying to separate my body parts from those of the truck this very minute!"

"First of all, from what little I know about explosives,

there isn't very much in the box. Most of what's in here are electronic circuit boards and other parts. Besides, if you had pressed your keyless entry device, say ten or fifteen feet away from your truck, like most people do, most of the damage would have been contained inside the truck."

The logic of this did not escape him and appeared to put him more at ease, so after giving the rest of the truck a good once-over, they decided to take their chances that no other booby traps existed. With fingers crossed, George turned the key, and both were pleased to hear the grind of the starter and the whir of the engine. George put the truck into gear, pulled slowly out of the parking place, trying the brakes and making sure the steering responded correctly.

They headed out of the airport parking lot and onto Highway 171 south towards Mansfield. The two-lane blacktop wound through rural Louisiana. Along the sides of the road were dense stands of pine trees. Some looked like virgin forest, others were definitely secondary growth as the young trees were interspersed between stumps remaining from previously harvested timber. From time to time, they saw fenced clearings with oil or gas derricks, some of which looked as if they had not operated in many years, crusted with rust and missing parts. Most of the homes they saw were pretty run-down, some with shabbily dressed children playing in what passed for a front yard. Occasionally, they came upon intersections of county roads where skeletons of gas stations and stores, a few turned into roadside churches advertising some obscure religious affiliation, beckoned to them. Once, in the middle of nowhere, a modern-looking gas station/liquor/convenience store appeared, its new concrete driveways at odds with the old dirt-covered pickup trucks and the multi-colored (and sometimes partially fendered) automobiles parked at the pumps. Some of the locals strutting their stuff, socializing and sharing a few cold ones before heading out on the road again. The weather which preceded their passing must have been rainy, as the ditches at the sides of the road were pretty full of water, muddied from the reddish colored clay that edged the ribbon of asphalt. Brad stared intently into the murky water, expecting to see a snake or alligator, but all he saw were a few white wading birds looking for a tasty meal of some hapless insect, and a hawk sitting on a fencepost, waiting for a mouse or other small rodent to scurry out from the foliage that bordered the shoulder of the road.

George suggested Brad watch for logging trucks, as they routinely used this route to carry the pine logs to the creosote plants, where they were treated under heat and pressure with a petroleum-based chemical which preserves the wood and discourages insect infestation and rot. He said Brad would understand his concern when we came upon one. The treated logs are then stored in huge piles and sold for railroad ties and fence posts. The same treatment was used for telephone and electric poles, however, they didn't see any trees large enough to be used for that purpose. It wasn't long until he saw one coming up behind them in his sideview mirror. They were doing the speed limit, but the truck was catching up like they were parked. It looked like the truck would run right over them, when at the last second, it pulled out and passed, nearly blowing them off the road. George nonchalantly mentioned that the more loads they deliver, the more money they make, and after they deliver a load, they flip the rear wheels and center support assembly "piggy back" on the truck cab and fly back up the road to the lumbering site to pick up another load, all at warp speed.

"You see a lot of the locals prefer driving on the shoulder to give the logging truck drivers plenty of room. You'll see a lot of white crosses on the side of the road, especially by curves and bridges," he observed, as he slowed while crossing another intersection with a county road. Brad noticed another log truck, without a load, waiting to pull out onto the tarmac. He spun his head around to look through the rear window as they passed the intersection. He watched the log truck make the turn onto their road with a cloud of dust, sand and loose gravel flying in a haze of diesel smoke belching from the twin chrome stacks on either side of its cab. On it came, just like the last one, except this time as he pulled out to go around them, the edge of his bumper caught their left rear quarter, turning them nearly broadside and forcing them onto the shoulder. As they slid sideways, half on and half off the road, Brad kept thinking how lucky they were not to have good enough traction to cause their truck to flip over and roll down the highway like a football. It probably took only minutes for them to come to a stop, but it seemed like an eternity until all movement ceased.

Brad's first concern was for his uncle. George still had his hands gripped tightly around the steering wheel and he stared straight ahead, looking but seeing nothing. There was no response when Brad asked if he was okay. He looked kind of pale and he made small rasping sounds as he breathed. Brad fumbled behind the seat back for his uncle's carry-on and as he searched its contents, he came up with what he was looking for: a bottle of whiskey. It amazed him how many people brought liquor when they traveled, as if they planned on a trip to someplace where it wasn't available. He opened the bottle and poured a small amount into his uncle's mouth. Whiskey running down his chin, he swallowed, gagged, choked and coughed, but the color returned to his cheeks and his eyes turned toward Brad with a sign of recognition. He released his grip on the steering wheel, reached out and took hold of the bottle. He took a long drink.

"Damn, that was close," he exclaimed, wiping his mouth with the back of his hand.

"Too close," Brad replied, reaching for the bottle.

"Not the truck," his uncle said, nodding toward the bottle in his hand. "I almost decided not to bring that with me!"

Laughing almost to the point of hysteria, Brad got out of the pickup to assess the damage. It looked a lot worse than it was. The wheels seemed to point in the right direction but he wouldn't have given much for the front end alignment. Miraculously, the tires still had air in them. Most of the body damage consisted of scratches and dents from bushes, branches and gravel. Nothing appeared to be leaking out from underneath. George had taken several generous swallows from the bottle and was beginning to feel its effects. He suggested that Brad drive, at least as far as Zwolle, about forty miles down the road, where they could get the truck checked out by a mechanic in the event it didn't run right.

When Brad tried to start the engine, it cranked and cranked but refused to start. He didn't remember his uncle shutting the key off after their near disaster and he said as much to him. George momentarily stopped nursing the whiskey bottle and giggled. Brad pulled the hood release, got back out of the truck and looked around under the hood. Nothing looked out of place or disconnected, but like most people would do under the same circumstances, he pushed everything that looked pushed-on and wiggled anything else that looked like an electrical connection. Stepping back into the pickup, he tried the key again, with the same result. He sat for a few moments, resting his forehead on the top edge of the steering wheel and tried to think back to an automotive class he had taken during one of his many semesters in college. He tried to think of a similar situation that his instructor might have described. Then, it came to him. He got back out and looked once more under the hood to verify that the engine was indeed fuel-injected. Finding that to be the case, he knelt down, and reached back to where the dashboard met the firewall at the edge of the floor carpeting. Pulling the carpeting slightly away he felt around for an object, probably a box with a button on it. As luck would have it, he found it on the first try and, feeling about, located the reset button. With a push of the button and a turn of the key, the engine cranked and suddenly roared to life. He stabbed the gas pedal a few times and the engine returned to a smooth idle.

"What did you do?" George asked, his words sounding slightly slurred.

"Fuel-injected vehicles, we learned in auto mechanics, use electric fuel pumps. In the event of an accident where the vehicle is rolled over or shaken about violently, a little box called a "rollover switch shuts the power off to the fuel pump to prevent gasoline from spraying out if a fuel line were to break, preventing an explosion or fire. By pushing the reset button, power is restored to the pump and poof . . . we're ready to go again."

Brad backed around and onto the highway, then proceeded slowly down the road, glancing at the gauges, testing the brakes and moving the steering wheel back and forth slightly to make sure everything responded the way it should. Several minutes later, he had accelerated to highway speeds and, not finding anything amiss, looked over at George to see how he was doing. He was slumped to his right, shoulder against the passenger side door, whiskey bottle cradled in his arm like a baby, and snoring with soft purring sounds.

Forty-five minutes later, they arrived in Zwolle without further incident. Going over a rather rough railroad crossing a few blocks into town woke George, who then directed Brad down the street they were on, right at the rear of the supermarket, following the curve past the creosote plant that spurted steam from the superheated chemicals, and down to the end of that road. They turned left on State Road 191. A few miles down, they passed over some small bridges and for the first time, they could see parts of the lake where rising water had formed small bays. Some of them were isolated from the main lake by the road, and others were accessible because the road was part of a bridge, providing clearance for boat traffic beneath it. It was just as Brad imagined it would be. Forests of tree remains of all sizes and shapes, some towering their naked branches twenty or more feet above the water, others only stumps showing their ragged tops above the choppy surface. Some leaned or were broken from the force of wind and waves and nestled against other trees.

"My goodness," he said, "every inch of water looks like prime bass fishing territory! How in the world do you know where to fish? I mean, there can't be fish everywhere, can there?"

His uncle reminded him that what they were driving over was only a very small part of Toledo Bend Reservoir and like any other lake, certain factors make some areas more attractive to bass than others. Because a majority of the water contained trees, the bass looked for other things besides trees. Possibly certain types of grass with the trees, certain depth with trees, access to deep water, bottom composition, shoreline, water temperature and a host of other factors. Their problem would be to try to determine where the bass would be under these conditions.

"But I'm sure you know most of that. That's why we pre-fish, to try and apply what we already know to this lake under today's conditions. By the way, as long as we're heading this way, we might as well stop at Tackle Town, a combination tackle store, restaurant and gas station. I need to make a pit stop, and we can pick up a fishing license for you and a lake map to study, just to help you get your bearings. It's real easy to get turned around and lost here." They approached an intersection where next to the stop sign was a marker indicating that a right turn would put them on County Road 6 to Pendelton Bridge, where Texas was across the way.

After stopping and looking all four ways at least four times and feeling like he should wait for some signal to proceed, Brad made sure his turn signal was flashing and turned to the right. Off to his right he saw a large commercial area with rows of pickup trucks and sport utilities with bass boats of every variety attached, parked on almost every available square foot of parking lot space. Without being told, he knew they had arrived at Tackle Town. He pulled into one of the few parking places that was not designed for a vehicle with a boat trailer, and Brad and his uncle got out of the cab, George hurrying ahead with that unmistakable sense of urgency—the step and facial expression of a man on a mission and a hope that the facility would not be "occupado."

The laugh that started in Brad's throat from watching his uncle's antics froze. Instead, a chill traveled down his spine as he glanced to his right. Off the rear corner of the gas station part of the building, he could see a logging truck. Even from where he was standing, he noticed that the bumper was damaged on the right side. He walked toward the truck, oblivious to everything but the wrinkled bumper, which he could now see had patches of red paint, the color of his uncle's pickup. The fact that the entire truck was covered with a thick layer of the reddish clay dirt, except for that particular area of the bumper, removed any doubt. This was the truck that had tried to run them off the road. He wondered what the truck was doing there. He wondered if the driver of that truck had tried on purpose to push them off the road or had only misjudged his maneuver, or if this incident was related to the bomb left in his uncle's truck earlier, or for that matter the strange occurrences at his boat factory. He wondered if he and his uncle were ever going to get to fish as the situation certainly seemed to be escalating, or if these were just random coincidences.

"Y'all lose somethin'?" drawled a voice from behind him.

Brad thought about a lie like looking for a restroom, but if this was the guy who drove that rig, he wasn't going to waste a lot of time playing the "dumb Yankee."

He wasn't going to be satisfied until one of them needed emergency medical treatment. Evidently, Bubba had the same idea because before Brad had a chance to come up with a response intended to antagonize him, a roundhouse right came straight for his ear. The body behind the fist was about two hundred pounds of logger muscle, plus about seventy-five pounds of beer belly hanging over wide belted Levis, clasped with a large brass buckle which proudly proclaimed Chevrolet "number one." He was well over six feet tall, including his baseball cap, which carried the same emblem as his belt buckle. His ruddy cheeks gave Brad the feeling that either this guy had high blood pressure or had been tipping a few cool ones. His gut feeling told him, if that punch landed, it would hurt, whether or not the man had been drinking.

Brad stepped into him close enough for the punch to miss his head, and he found, from the man's breath, that he probably didn't have high blood pressure. Brad grabbed the man's extended arm and let his force and weight carry him forward until he was off balance, then Brad, turning and swinging his right elbow into the area under the man's armpit, dropped him to the ground, clutching his sore ribs. He was faster than Brad would have given him credit for, and was on his knees in an instant, shaking off the pain. In the movies, the actors get kicked, punched and hit over the head with solid objects and still get up to fight with hardly a sign of any injury. This guy was going to have one hell of a black and blue mark on his side below his armpit and quite possibly a cracked rib or two. He was also mad as hell. Although Brad thought himself the good guy, no way was he about to let this big guy get up and try again. Brad kicked him in the solar plexus, and unlike movie heroes, Bubba fell to his back making short gasping noises, while his arms and legs twitched uncontrollably. Brad walked over to the gas station and picked up a length of water hose coiled by the side of the building. He dragged it back to where Bubba still lay and sprayed him with water until he began to come around. Eventually, his eyes focused and he tried to lift his arms to deflect the water from his face. The big man got slowly to his knees, and Brad had the feeling the man still had some fight left in him. Brad took hold of him by the front of his shirt and helped lift him to an almost upright position. Then, with the heel of his hand, Brad hit him squarely on the nose, just hard enough to break it but not hard enough to drive the cartilage back into his brain and kill him. Brad hoped the pain and copious amounts of blood from a shattered nose would be enough to take this guy's mind off of fighting.

"You're gonna kill me," Bubba wailed, his voice shrill with panic.

"Now, you're getting the idea," Brad replied. "After all, turnabout is fair play. You tried to kill us with your truck a few miles back, now it's my turn."

"Please, mister . . . please! don't kill—" he choked and sobbed.

Brad had no intention of killing the man, but he wanted him to be very afraid of the possibility. If the truck incident wasn't a random act, which Brad suspected it wasn't, he wanted to find out who was responsible.

"Let's have a little talk, then. Who put you up to this? And don't try to tell me you're just a lousy driver, you have a lot more parts left to break."

"No . . . please! I don't know who the guy was, I swear! I was in a bar about a mile back from where I pulled out behind you fellas. I was havin' a few beers during my lunch break from haulin' logs, when this guy I'd never seen before comes over to me and starts buyin' me drinks. He don't look like no fag so I figure, what the hell? Next thing I know, he starts telling me how I look like I could handle myself pretty good and would I be interested in making some easy money? He told me he was just trying to scare the hell out of someone. He told me what kind of pickup to look for. He said I was to sit at the bar until he called and then wait at the crossroad until I saw the truck come by. Then I was to run it off the road, making it look like an accident. He gave me enough money to have my truck fixed and a lot more besides. He told me to have my truck fixed right away so no one could tell who did it. That's why I come to this here garage. It was more money than I could make runnin' logs for a week . . . he . . . he said he was just tryin' to scare you guys."

Once started, he kept blubbering, mostly incoherently, bleeding all the while. Brad knew Bubba wasn't smart enough to be making up the story, so he warned him in his most threatening voice, never to cross his path again. Brad started to walk away, then he turned to take a last look at the hulk of a man he had reduced to a sobbing, wheezing blob, and his heart went out to him. It was true, he and his uncle could have been killed and he had little doubt, had it not been for his defensive skills the man would have beaten him mercilessly. Still, he had never had occasion to hurt another human being that severely and while it felt good when the adrenaline was pumping, pangs of conscience now gnawed at him. He walked back over to where the man still kneeled, hands covering rapidly swelling features, blood trickling from between fat fingers, helped him to his feet and walked him to his truck. Feeling somewhat less guilty, Brad started back across the parking lot to find his uncle. He couldn't help but thinking that a week of hauling logs would have been easier for Bubba. While he walked, he tried to make sense of what had happened. Some strange things had happened to his uncle which may or may not have been coincidence. The bomb had to have been put in his uncle's truck by someone who knew his itinerary. They had been run off the road, supposedly as a warning. If someone was trying to scare them, they were doing a good job, but he wondered what the warning was supposed to be. As he came around the front of the tackle shop, his uncle was coming out of the door, his arms full of bags.

"I've been looking for you," his uncle said. "You have to sign for your fishing license. Where've you been?"

"Having a nice conversation with the driver of the logging truck that tried to run us off the road back there," Brad replied.

"You what? Where? How? What happened?" his uncle sputtered.

"I'll skip the blow-by-blow description, but I found out it was no accident. Someone paid him to scare us. And I'll bet it was the same person responsible for the bomb in your truck. What still doesn't make sense is what any of this has to do with boat secrets. I'm getting some pretty mixed messages. Maybe I'm just not clever enough to see a pattern here."

His uncle stood listening, his eyes wide and his mouth opening and closing with no sound coming out. Finally he stammered, "I'll be doggone, if you don't have a way! See here, a total stranger tries to make us a permanent part of the landscape, you just happen to run into him in the parking lot and he tells you the whole story. What did you do, walk up, introduce yourself and ask him why he tried to kill us, thank him and walk him arm-in-arm back to his truck?"

"Actually," Brad said, "that's pretty much the way it happened. I did have to convince him first, however, if he ever wanted to make the two-tooth minimum in his favorite bar again, he'd better talk."

"I miss all the fun," his uncle said with a shake of his head.

2

Feeling better, his Uncle George got behind the wheel again, heading them down the road toward Pendelton Bridge. The road had a slight but noticeable incline and soon Brad could see where the bridge began, but try as he might, he could not see the other end. He said as much to his uncle, who chuckled, telling him he was not surprised, since the bridge was four miles long. He said that the bridge was actually built on top of an old bridge that spanned the river before the lake was filled.

"There's some great crappie fishing this time of the year around the bridge supports," his uncle said. "You'll see boats anchored or tied between the spans, so we'll have to be careful running under the bridge. You can sometimes pick up some nice bass off the pilings near the shore. We should be able to see the red and green channel markers that mark the north/south boat lanes. The easiest way to get from the Texas to the Louisiana side when you're on the water around here is to run on either side of the bridge. They've cleared the stumps along both sides of the bridge when they built it. Also, if the wind comes up and you need to cross, the bridge helps block the waves. This bridge is almost the exact middle of the lake, and divides it north and south."

Driving across the low sided concrete ribbon, the view was spectacular. As far as Brad could see, the entire surface of the water was dotted with trees and stumps of every size and shape. Some of the trunks still held their bark, while others were bare, bleached silver by the action of wind and waves. He remembered an old guide he had had once on Beaver Lake in Arkansas, who said that every tree held a bass. He decided, if that were only half true, he could understand why Toledo Bend had the reputation it did. He was only partially listening to his uncle's lake chatter, as his thoughts kept returning to the events of the past few hours. The only pattern he could see was that the way things were escalating, there appeared to be a sense of urgency.

"Can you think of anything coming up soon that would cause whoever is responsible for our 'accidents' to be stepping up the pace?"

"Not really. A couple of boat shows, the fishing tournament . . . I don't know. This is our busiest time of the year," George mused. "Besides building the boats for dealer's stock and last year's orders, the spring boat shows usually bring additional orders. If need-be, this is the time when I become the research and development department. If the competition is showing something new and different and softening our sales, I try to upgrade our products, as long as it doesn't compromise our commitment to quality or safety. In the meantime, I putter with some new materials that I hear about in industrial synthetics magazines, but anybody has the same access to that stuff as I do. I'm constantly trying to improve our manufacturing system. I've developed a system for tracking exactly who does what. If a boat comes back to the factory for a specific problem, or if a dealer complains of something quality-related, I can trace it back to the worker who was responsible. If it turns out to be poor workmanship, the repair time is deducted from that worker's pay. Too many deductions in a given period, and they're history."

"That's very interesting," Brad reflected. "It also puts

another spin on our problem. Suppose what's been going on is just plain old-fashioned revenge. What if a disgruntled former employee with a weird sense of justice is trying to get even? In any case, we're going to have to watch our 'back trail.' We still don't know with what or whom we're dealing. Our disadvantage is that we don't know what direction or form the next attempt might take. It's going to be a continuous distraction. We've been lucky so far, but with the pace picking up, it's going to be more difficult to defend ourselves against another 'accident.' I'm afraid we won't be much competition in the tournament if we can't concentrate totally on fishing." He thought for a moment. "Say, maybe that's the plan, to make sure we don't win the fishing tournament."

"Don't jump to any conclusions," George countered. "There are hundreds of tournaments on this lake every year, and I haven't won one yet. I don't think I'm much of a threat, besides there's not all that much at stake here. But I've given some thought to what you said about being distracted. Out on the water all day will make it more difficult for anyone to sneak up on us, but, it will leave my house and factory unprotected. Don't forget, only the two of us know where we will be fishing, and with the size of the reservoir, following us wouldn't be very practical. Anyone trying to approach us would almost have to stay in the boat lanes, making them highly visible. I keep a gun in my boat loaded with 'rat shot' in case I come across a very aggressive snake or gator, but I'll bring some regular bullets, just in case. That leaves going home at night. Let's stop at the factory on the way. I'll show you the rig we'll be using, and you can take a quick look around while nobody's working. Now, let's try and pretend nothing's happened, and spend the rest of the evening looking over the lake maps and deciding which baits to try."

They crossed the bridge and Brad saw the signs at the side of the road. "Welcome to Texas," followed by "Buckle Up" and "The eyes of Texas are upon you—Don't litter," then a variety of billboards advertising supper clubs and boat and motor repair shops, probably a valuable commodity on a lake like Toledo Bend.

The two-lane country road they turned onto wound its way through some of the most beautiful scenery he had seen thus far. The grass was green and lush. Pine, oak and cedar trees grew thick. It was easy for him to visualize how the area might have looked before it flooded. Vast grassy flats giving way to humps of trees and brush, here and there a run-down house or mobile home. He thought that there were probably many houses under the water, or at least the foundations, which would make good structure for holding fish. He hoped his uncle had a good locator on his boat. Wildflowers grew in clumps where it was obvious that no attempts at landscaping had been made. They had driven several miles when Brad caught glimpses of what looked like other lakes through the trees and beyond the ridges. His uncle assured him that what he was seeing was still part of the Toledo Bend Reservoir. Captivated as he was by the beauty of the scenery, Brad was reminded of the disregard some people had for the delicate balance of nature by the rusted hulks of old cars and pickup trucks in yards, fields and along the side of houses, old tires and colleagues of rotten wood and metal, with an occasional plastic bag full of garbage. Brad thought how the users and the spoilers still looked upon nature as a dumping ground. If left alone, they would bury themselves in their own refuse, pollute the air and water, and blame it on somebody else.

A large sign read "Caliente Peformance Boats," with a picture of a speeding bass boat in the middle, over an arrow with the words ONE MILE inside, indicating a left turn.

"Not much farther now," his Uncle George said, interrupting his thoughts. "Less than a mile down this road. We've got about thirty-five acres, over five-hundred feet of lake frontage with our own boat ramp. I like to water-test all our boats before they leave the factory. This way, we can also ensure proper propeller selection, since no two hulls react exactly alike."

They both saw it at the same time. Smoke still smoldered from the rubble. What was left of the wooden truss roof was lying on what was left of everything else, like adding logs to a fire. While fiberglass itself will not burn, it will support combustion, and if hot enough, melt into an unrecognizable mess. Very little was left to remind anyone of the thriving business that existed only hours ago. They rolled slowly to a stop and stepped out of the truck. Off to the left stood a smaller building that looked like a garage and was obviously untouched by the inferno. It had three overhead doors, the middle one having a small passage door that could swing open without lifting the entire door. The smaller door opened, a man stepped out and started toward them. He held what looked like a shotgun in his hands, pointed a little too casually in their direction. He looked from Brad to his uncle, recognition coming slowly to his bloodshot eyes. He lowered the gun. Wet gravel and charred residue crunched beneath their shoes, raising small puffs which seemed strangely out of place, considering the amount of water left from the inadequate efforts of the volunteer fire department. George walked up to the man taking his right hand and putting his left arm around his shoulders.

"Brad, this here is Jim Taylor. Most folks just call him "Jimbo." Jimbo, meet my nephew, Brad Allen. Jimbo is my foreman, my right hand man, and a good fishing buddy."

Brad could easily understand why people called him Jimbo. He was the biggest man he'd ever seen. There hadn't been many men he had had to look up to, in order to look them in the eyes. Jimbo must have been over six-foot-six, and at least two hundred and fifty pounds. What he could see behind his bib overalls looked like solid muscle, and beneath the worn cap with a barely readable "Mann's Baits" was a lined, tanned face with a friendly smile. He could have been forty or sixty. In either case, he didn't think he'd care to try to make him go north if he was headed south. Jimbo stood the shotgun butt on the top of his boot and rested the barrel against his thigh as he reached out a massive hand toward Brad and without squeezing, engulfed Brad's right hand and shook it firmly.

"Pleased to meet you," Jimbo said sincerely. Jimbo knew that George had gone north to his brother's funeral, and was not surprised that he had brought his nephew back with him. He knew, perhaps better than anyone, the rejuvenating effect the area could have.

"I talked Brad into coming back with me to fish the tournament this weekend. I had an idea he might like to look around the boat factory, and maybe stay on and work with us, but now . . . " George trailed off with a catch in his voice.

It might have been the smoke that still lingered in the air, but Brad swore he could see tears forming in his uncle's eyes.

"You know," he said to Jimbo and Brad, looking at the rubble but not really seeing it. "When everything goes smoothly and comes out right, they call you a 'visionary' and a 'leader,' but when things turn to shit, they say you're just an old fool! What happened here, Jimbo?"

"Honestly, Boss, I don't rightly know. Yesterday bein'

Saturday, I came by afore noon to check things out, like usual. You know, makin' sure the crew didn't leave any dirty chop guns or open resin out, and checkin' the plugs to see if they were curin' okay. I always feel better when I know we can come in Monday morning and have no surprises. Everything looked normal, so I checked the window and door locks because of how you been worried about someone breakin' in. Then, I went out to the garage to check the tournament rig you was workin' on out there. Seein' everythin' looked all right, I locked up and went home. My phone rang early this mornin'. It was the sheriff tellin' me to get my butt over here pronto, as all hell was bustin' loose. I jumped in my pickup and beat it over here. The fire department, sheriff, county and state police were all over the place. Seems they was worried about toxic chemical fumes or toxic waste getting into the lake. By the time I got here, the roof had already come down and even with them pumpin' water out of the lake, well, this is all that's left. They sprayed lots of water on the garage to keep the fire from spreadin' over to it, too. That's how I come to be here this afternoon when you boys showed up. I stayed to make sure nothin' was water damaged or gotten into durin' all the excitement. When I heard your truck pull up, I didn't recognize it all beat-up and dirty. . . . Say, what happened to it, anyway?"

"It's a long story," said Uncle George, "I'll tell you about it when we're out on the water pre-fishing. Go ahead with what you were saying."

"Well . . . there ain't much more, as I said, when I didn't recognize your truck and two guys got out, I thought you might be looters or somethin', so I got down one of them old shotguns we used to take duck huntin', and here we are."

"I'm sure glad you didn't shoot first and ask questions

after," Brad interjected.

"Lord, it ain't even loaded." A smile broke the lines on Jimbo's face into a road map.

"Tell me, Jimbo," Uncle George pleaded, "was it an accident, or did someone set it on fire?"

"As God is my witness, I don't know! But why on earth would anybody want to burn us out?"

"Well, I'm sure as hell going to find out if it's the last thing I do!"

They told Jimbo to meet them at the boat ramp at first light, watched him open one of the large overhead doors of the garage, back his old pickup out, close and lock the door, and drive away.

Brad wanted to walk around the property to look for some sort of clue. He also wanted a chance to think and to try putting some pieces of this puzzle together before more damage was done and somebody got hurt. Uncle George walked back into the garage and Brad made his way down to the boat ramp area.

The boat ramp was actually a well-built concrete affair with raised edges to prevent erosion and deep ribs to improve traction when the ramp got wet or slippery with algae growth. Like all good ramps, it had a steep drop-off at the point where the boat would float off the trailer before the rear wheels of the tow vehicle reached the water. At the side of the ramp was a solid-looking dock made of treated lumber on large foam floats, so it could go up and down as the water level varied. All sharp edges were well-cushioned with vinyl molding or inflatable bumpers, all strategically placed to protect any boat attempting to approach the dock. Uncle George was taking no chance of scratching a new boat after a water test.

From the boat ramp, the road turned to gravel, leading up toward the remains of the factory. Brad looked all about for anything unusual. There were lots of shoe and boot impressions in the mud and grass, no doubt belonging to the police and firefighters. Then, on the deck of the boat dock, he saw muddy footprints. At first he almost ignored them, but examining them more closely, he noticed they headed toward the water as if someone had returned to a boat after walking in mud. But more importantly, he could still see the imprint of the shoe manufacturer in the mud. It was a custom made shoe, only available by mail order and very expensive, hardly the kind of shoe likely to be worn by police or firemen. He carefully scraped up one clump of the hardened muddy prints, wrapped it in his handkerchief and put it in his jacket pocket. He made a mental note to ask his uncle if he knew anybody who wore those kind of shoes. Nothing else looked suspicious, so he walked up and began to systematically climb through the remains, some of which were still smoldering. One thing that bothered him was the appearance that the building was quickly consumed. But that could be explained by the chemicals used in the fiberglass process. He would have to ask about that, too.

He could see that the floor was made of concrete with stub walls of block extending up about two feet. The side supports and the roof trusses must have been southern yellow pine or western larch covered with corrugated metal sheeting. Almost no trace of the wood was left, which he thought indicated a type of wood with a lot of sap rather than a dry wood, as the building wasn't old enough for the wood to have dried that much. Also, sappy wood would burn hotter and from the condition of the remnants of metal sheeting, twisted and melted in places, the fire must have been extraordinarily hot. Small pieces of gypsum board, along with fused and melted remains of wire and electrical fittings suggested interior partition walls. Possibly a few small offices and a restroom. He suspected if he dug around a bit, he could find pieces of a toilet and lavatory Being made of porcelain, they would not have burned.

In an area along what was once an outside wall, he found the remains of large metal drums which probably held resins, hardener and solvents. Nearby were what must have been rolls of fiberglass cloth and mat. Most of the outer layers were badly melted, but he thought the inside would most likely still be usable. What seemed to him most curious was that one area, near the center, looked relatively free of debris, almost as if everything exploded out from that point. He wondered if the local authorities would investigate this fire as being suspicious in nature, or consider it an act of God based on the type of chemicals used in boat manufacturing. Perhaps they needed to consider sharing their experiences with the local police, of whom he had seen no sign. He had seen many television shows and movies depicting the antics of small town sheriffs and police, and he supposed he would be hesitant to involve them.

Finding nothing more of interest, he walked over to the garage where George was sitting behind a desk in an office that made up the garage's other half. In one corner stood several tall filing cabinets. On the desk were the usual desk items, but looking rather out-of-place in this setting were a computer, printer and what looked like a scanner.

Apparently, the look on his face prompted his uncle to ask, "Do you think we still write on clay tablets? We may be out in the boonies, but we still enjoy some of the benefits of civilization. I even have a program that lets me simulate hull stresses under real-time conditions without actually building or putting one in water. Don't look so surprised, computers save a whole lot of trial and error; they're very cost-effective."

"Tell me about Jimbo," Brad said, shifting uneasily from side to side and trying not to look as foolish as he felt.

"Jimbo just appeared about eighteen years ago, walked up to me and asked for a job, said he'd do anything as long as it was legal. I had only been in business a short while and needed all sorts of help. Jimbo caught on real quick. After a while, he could do any job he was shown and usually better than anybody. What's more, the other workers liked him, kind of looked up to him, not because he was bigger and stronger, but because he seemed to intuitively do and say the right things. He was always able to simplify things, break them down to understandable and manageable proportions. Whatever job he was doing at the time, he always got right down to the cause of a problem, even in another area. He could see the big picture and put things in perspective. I believe if he had had the education and opportunity, he could have been or done anything he put his mind to. Yet, he's totally happy doing exactly what he does. He sort of became foreman by consensus. I couldn't imagine it any other way. I would trust him with my life. I know he's been offered higher-paying jobs, but he says I trusted him when he needed me and he'll stay with me as long as I need him. You can't ask for more loyalty then that. Besides, he's gotten to know every guide on The Bend, and knows more about fishing patterns than most of them. With his help, we could win this tournament."

"How can you think of fishing with all that's happened?" Brad asked.

"I thought you were a fisherman! What's a few attempts on my life and burning down my business got to do with fishing? After all, it will be at least a week until the insurance adjusters get around to looking things over. Sitting around worrying about what's happened isn't going to undo anything! Nothing like a few days of good bass fishing to take your mind off trouble. Now forget about being a detective and come look at our rig."

They went over to the other side of the garage, Uncle George in the lead so that Brad's view was somewhat obscured by his body. As he moved to the side, Brad was looking at the most beautiful bass boat he had ever seen. It was a full twenty feet long, and noticeably wider than most others. The inlays and multicolored graphics were set off by the red carpeting melting into metal-flake red, changing into electric blue as it traveled down the breadth of the hull. The trailer was painted with matching graphics and four beautiful alloy rims and fancy tires. The engine was one of the major brands and advertised 225 horsepower, but Uncle George said that he had it modified to produce nearly three hundred. He went on to tell Brad that the hull was made from a new composite fiberglass-graphite-polycarbonate material which was stronger and tougher, yet lighter by half than other boats of similar size. Unlike traditional fiberglass, with gel coats that can crack and craze from impacts, this new material had no gel coat or separate layers. The composites formed a glossy smooth surface with the strength and flexibility of built-up layers of cloth and mat. The colors and metal-flake were added from the inside during the molding process and worked their way through, so that they could be seen from the outside after curing. The hull looked brand new but Uncle George assured Brad he had used it for nearly five hundred hours of running time in the stump-filled waters, with no sign of even minor scratches. He admitted that these new materials were as yet too expensive and would need extensive further testing, but they were going to have one hell of a ride.

After gathering from the file cabinets and a computer disk storage box materials he would need to furnish the insurance company, Uncle George checked to see that all of the doors and windows were secured, walked back up to the battered pickup truck, and headed back down the road to his house.

The house wasn't at all what Brad expected, although he was not sure exactly what he had expected. In all of the areas they drove through, the permanent houses were mainly of wood-frame construction, with no foundations, and generally run-down in appearance. Some had windows missing or broken, doors standing ajar or gone altogether, and all sorely in need of paint and basic lawn care. The nicer homes, it appeared, were mobile homes set on concrete slabs in the middle of well-manicured lawns. Brad did notice something both types had in common: a fairly late model pickup truck and bass boat in the driveway. He guessed when one lived close to a body of water like Toledo Bend, as Uncle George indicated, it was a matter of priorities.

The driveway they pulled into led up to a neat suburban-style brick ranch. There was nothing pretentious about it. It would have fit unobtrusively into any neighborhood. It looked comfortable and out of place. They parked the truck in front of the nearest door on the attached two-car garage. Brad suggested to his Uncle George that he wait in the truck while he took a walk around the house and checked things out. He pointed out that they had had too many "accidents" already. His uncle readily agreed, so he got out and started strolling around from front to back, not having the slightest idea what he was looking for.

Mats of pine needles cushioned his steps while every now and then the crunch of a small pine cone froze his forward progress. Around the back yard, the sweet smell of vanilla from the bark of the pines reminded him they hadn't eaten since breakfast. They had intended to get some lunch at the tackle store/restaurant/gas station but Brad's encounter with Bubba took his mind off of his appetite. He looked for signs of forced entry on each window and the sliding glass doors which opened onto a redwood deck in the back yard with its view of jack-in-the-pulpit, May apple and trillium blooms, forming a natural border between the yard and a thick stand of pines. Large groupings of columbine and lady-slippers contrasted the white delicate blooms of hepatica. Garden variety annuals could never hope to compete with the natural beauty of wildflowers. Many self-proclaimed gardeners would tear them out by the roots to make room for rose bushes or pansies, and developers would bulldoze vast acres to make construction of matchbox houses easier, sterilizing the ground so nothing as mundane as a wildflower could dare grow through the sod. Brad didn't think his uncle was a wildflower fancier; it was more likely through neglect and close proximity to the woods that they took over.

He found himself back where he started, but before pronouncing it safe to enter, he looked through the side window into the garage. The side in front of which they had parked was empty; however, sitting in the other bay was another bass boat. It looked like an older style, but in excellent condition.

"That is the first boat finished from my factory," sighed Uncle George as he came around the rear of the truck, fumbling for his house key. "The hull was molded from a used plug I bought from another manufacturer. Building plugs is the most expensive part of the process and ideally, they should only be used a limited number of times to produce the best quality finish. Consequently, larger outfits oftentimes sell their older, usable plugs to smaller or newer outfits, like I was twenty years ago. That was a long time ago. Lately, we've been selling our plugs to other boat builders. Jimbo is in charge of building ours . . . was . . . until . . . now."

"Here, let me," Brad insisted, as he took the keys from his uncle's hand and, after a few tries, fitted the right one into the lock. The lock turned smoothly and Uncle George said, "Let me go in first and get the lights, so you don't trip over anything. Living alone, I'm not much of a housekeeper and I left in kind of a hurry."

As Brad pushed open the door and stepped back out of his uncle's way, a strangely familiar odor reached his nostrils. He quickly shot out his hand and grabbed for any part of his uncle that he could find, given the awkwardness of his position, and pulled. When he put his hand on someone or something, it usually moved. Likewise his uncle came flying out of the doorway, landing almost in the middle of the front lawn in a confused heap.

"What the . . . Who the . . . Are you crazy?" he gasped.

"I'll apologize later, Unc. Stay right where you are and don't move a muscle," Brad yelled, but he was already halfway around the back of the house. With a short leap, he cleared the fence surrounding the large propane tank at the far end of the yard, and opening the cover over the pressure regulator valve, closed it tightly. Then he walked on a straight line to the rear of the house where he hoped the supply line, buried in the yard, came up to go through the wall and into the house. Sure enough, he found the small diameter copper pipe coming out of the ground and disappearing through thc wall. Giving it a slight tug, it easily came out of the wall and Brad could see the marks where it had been cut and pushed back into the house.

The sun had been going down for a while and by the time Brad got back to where his uncle still lay in the middle of the lawn, he could no longer recognize his features. Hearing his approach, the unmistakable voice said, "Would you please tell me what the hell is going on here? I think you fractured my shoulder."

"We need to very carefully open all of the windows and doors in your house without turning on any lights or touching anything that's liable to create a spark. If you left the furnace or air conditioning on automatic I'll have to shut off the main electrical breaker so it cannot come on. The house is full of propane gas fumes and any spark, no matter how small, could make your house rubble, just like your factory, and it could take your neighbor's houses with it, too."

Brad found the circuit breaker box in the garage and, just to make sure, shut off all of the electricity in the house, while his uncle went through the house opening all of the windows and doors. Fortunately, his house had no basement as propane gas, being heavier than air would never have gotten out by itself and fans or blowers would have been needed to force it up and out.

They sat together once again in the pickup, waiting for the fumes to clear out of the house. Brad sensed his uncle's nerves were stretched pretty tight after all that had happened today and he said, "I'm getting to feel real comfortable in this truck seat."

"Did you have to turn off all the electricity in the house?"

"I didn't have to, but it was the safest thing to do. Why do you ask?"

"Damn, now I have to reprogram my VCR," Uncle

George replied with the most serious "deadpan" expression he could manage.

Seeing the look on his face by the glow of the dome light from the roof of the cab, and expecting some "woe is me" comment from his uncle, the VCR statement totally unhinged Brad. As the last rays of the sun left the final visages of the house and trees, the sound of outrageous laughter stilled the music of the crickets and the croak of the frogs, once again Brad and his uncle found release, with some help from the bottle.

After a reasonable length of time, aided by a lively evening breeze, they were able to enter George's house. Brad went into the garage and reset the main breaker, restoring electrical power to the house. As he walked from the garage to the house, Brad saw first one, then another light go on and, entering the front door, he saw his uncle kneeling in front of the television set, playing with the VCR.

"Why do they make it so damned complicated to program a VCR? It shouldn't be harder than brain surgery."

"Uncle George, do you have any tools around the house? I thought I'd repair that copper propane line so we can cook, have heat and hot water for showers."

"Brad, I think it's time we involve the law. I'm going to call the sheriff before you fix anything. This has gone far enough. We may not be as lucky the next time, and now I'm sure there will be a next time."

3

Uncle George dialed the phone while Brad looked through kitchen cabinets and the refrigerator for something to eat. While he munched on soggy crackers and a cheese that gave new meaning to the word "aged," he listened to the conversation between his uncle and someone named Pat. George was telling Pat all of the events leading up to this evening. He said he and his nephew would be home all evening and yes, he would appreciate very much a visit tonight. Hanging up the phone, he reached for the crackers and indicated that the sheriff would be right over.

"Tell me about the local law," Brad said. "I can't help but expect a cross between Enos from *The Dukes Of Hazzard* and Andy of Mayberry."

"You've been watching too much television," Uncle George replied. "Wait and see."

Ten minutes later, the doorbell rang. George opened the door and stood aside. Brad turned in time to see Sheriff Pat, which he quickly figured out was short for Patricia, step through the doorway and enter the living room. She was tall, at least five-foot-ten. She was dressed in what looked like the generic mail-order variety law enforcement uniform. The next size larger would have looked "baggy," and the next size smaller would have been lurid. The size she wore needed more room in places where she was generously endowed. Her holstered gun stood almost straight out to the side due to her narrow waist and the flare of her hips. The pens and pencil in her shirt pocket lay nearly flat on her ample bosom. To say she was beautiful, Brad would have had to reevaluate his taste in women. To say she was average-looking would have been an understatement as there was much more of her than the average man could possibly handle. Her facial features were definitely feminine, but Brad would have described her as "handsome" rather than "beautiful." Her long red hair was loosely gathered to fit under her hat. At first, Brad thought she had a nice tan for someone who wore a uniform all day, but he decided her honey colored skin was most likely genetic, possibly Cajun. He guessed she was in her late twenties or early thirties, but he never had been very good at estimating women's ages.

Uncle George made the necessary introductions, and Brad reached out to her. Her hand was large, and her long tapering fingers were in perfect proportion. She wore her unpolished fingernails unfashionably short. Brad took her hand and locked her eyes with his gaze.

For the first time in her life, Pat felt weak. Her legs turned to rubber and she had to make a conscious effort to remain standing. Every atom in her body wanted to sink to the floor in a swoon. This couldn't be happening, she thought. She was no lovesick little girl and he certainly wasn't "drop dead" handsome. Still, his brown eyes were not plain, but the brightest, shiniest she had ever seen, and they were in sharp contrast with the white around them.

Brad couldn't explain why, but he looked to see that she wore no wedding ring. She radiated an aura of strength. Brad felt that she would be overpowering, physically and sexually. That feeling instantly stirred a desire within him that made him feel uncomfortable. It was not that he had never had those feelings before, it was just that he had never felt such power emanating from one person. It affected him deeply. When she spoke, her voice seemed to penetrate to his very core. Not sure of what was happening inside him, Brad decided that all of the recent experiences had left his emotions raw, and his reactions and feelings more intense. Releasing each other's hand was like breaking a high-voltage electrical connection. Later, he would swear something like a spark continued to flow as their fingers separated.

"Your uncle told me he thinks someone's trying to kill him, and maybe you, too." Pat said this matter-of-factly.

Brad just nodded. He loved the inflections of her subtle Cajun accent. He never tired of listening to them talk. He had had a friend in college who was from Louisiana, and no matter what his friend had to say, it always sounded happy and carefree. They used to sit and talk for hours, Brad mostly listened to the stories his friend told of fishing and hunting in the backwaters and bayous. Sometimes the stories were outrageous, with unbelievable endings, but when he finished telling the tale, they both laughed and laughed.

One story in particular came to mind. It concerned a fishing trip his friend had taken to a fairly new reservoir by Baton Rouge. It seemed the reservoir sat in a low area, covering what used to be part of an old automobile graveyard. The water was so clear, one could see the old cars piled up, some within inches of the surface. The wrecks were left, as they figured it would make good structure for the bass. They went out in an old "John" boat and cast around the edges of the sunken cars, each one acting like a small drop-off. All at once, his friend got the telltale "tap tap," lowered his rod tip, reeled the slack from the line, reared back and "crossed his eyes. The fish jumped once and began a run. His friend got a good look at the fish, and figured it weighed at least fifteen pounds. He described how the fish went around the boat, under the boat, and finally dove right through an open window of an old pickup truck about a foot below the surface of the water. Try as he might, he could not get that fish to come loose from the inside of that truck. He was afraid to pull too hard, for fear of breaking the line or cutting it on some hang-up inside the cab. His friend said he had lain down flat in the bottom of the boat, reaching down as far as he could, sliding his hand along the line to try and lip the bass or at least "catch him loose" from inside the truck. Part of the time his head was under the water, and as he built the tension to the max, his friend said, "Then what you think happen? That old mamma hawg, she roll the window up on my arm, so I like to near drown to death." With that, he laughed hysterically.

Brad immediately warmed to the sheriff. He wanted her to go on talking, and he was afraid if he said anything, the spell would be broken.

"He told me over the phone what happened to you both today'" she went on. "I'd like to hear your version, in your own words. If you don't mind, I'm going to record your story on this small cassette recorder, so I won't forget any of it."

She pushed the button to "record" and identified herself, the date and the time of day. She identified Brad and his uncle and the home address. Then she motioned to Brad to begin his narration. He began by telling her what his uncle had told him before they got on the plane. About the strange happenings at his factory during the preceding weeks. Then he described to her in great detail everything that occurred from the time they got off the airplane until just before she walked in the door. He told her about the bomb in the pickup truck, then excused himself for a few minutes to go out to his uncle's truck to retrieve the bomb from behind the seat. He took the time to bring the two carry-ons into the house, as they were forgotten in all of the excitement. He removed the cover and showed Pat the contents of the black box, while trying to explain in simple terms how he thought the device worked.

Evidently, she was convinced he was right about it being a bomb, because she appeared quite nervous until Brad offered to take it out to the garage She said that in the morning she would call the nearest agency that had a bomb disposal unit and have them come by and pick it up.

He told her about the logging truck and his encounter with the driver at Tackle Town. Pat asked him for a detailed description of Bubba and if he would have some time after pre-fishing tomorrow to come in and look through some mug shots. It was quite possible Bubba could have a rap sheet.

After he described the short, and rather one-sided altercation in the parking lot, she looked Brad over once again, and this time her eyes moved over him more slowly. The way her tongue played with the edge her lip and her jaw tightened made Brad feel even more uncomfortable. He smiled sheepishly, told her about his searching around the factory fire, and showed her the dried mud footprint from his jacket pocket. He finished his story by showing her the cut copper propane line and explaining how he discovered it. He left out his fear, his anxiety and the bottle of whiskey he and George had consumed to calm their nerves.

She shut off the recorder and stared at him. He could see a tiny wet spot in the little hollow at the base of her neck. He wasn't sure, but he thought she was breathing a bit faster. Her silence was unnerving.

"You've been a busy boy," she said, breaking the tension in the air. "You're either the luckiest man alive, or I should be working for you," she added. "I'll call Ron over at ProGas in the morning, and get him out here to repair the propane line. While he's at it, I'll have him check the whole system and all of the appliances, just to make sure. Then I'll get over to the factory and look around, and I'll detail my deputy to make extra rounds by the house and what's left out at the factory. Unfortunately, we don't have a lot to go on, and all of this is a bit more than I'm trained to deal with. But from what you've told me, I believe the two of you are in real danger. I'll do everything I can to help, but in the meantime, if either of you think of anything that might be of further help in figuring out who's behind this, give me a call. And Brad, don't forget to come into the office sometime tomorrow to look at some pictures. Maybe we'll find your friend from the gas station."

With that, they said goodbye and watched her walk out the door. Brad thought to himself that she looked even better from the back. A few seconds later he heard the sound of her car start, back out of the driveway and take off down the road.

"Was it as good for you as it was for her?" his uncle asked, tilting his head to one side with a knowing look on his face. "I never saw so much action with so little movement. That handshake made me feel as embarrassed as if I accidentally walked in on my parents having sex."

"I don't know what you're talking about," said Brad, but the mere mention of sex brought a flush to his face and a stirring in his being that was alien to him. He couldn't deny that there was a definite connection between them, but at such an unlikely time and under such unlikely circumstances he didn't fully understand his feelings.

“I’m really very tired, Uncle George. Just show me where, and I think I’ll turn in.”

“It’s not surprising, I’m sure,” his uncle replied. “You wouldn’t like a cigarette after . . . ”

“Just leave it alone,” Brad snapped back, with a grin which said that it had been a moving experience for him as well.

Five o’clock in the morning came all too soon for Brad as he sat up in his bed and looked out of the window, only to find it was still dark. He had spent a restless night lost in the convoluted fact and fiction of his dreams. He was being chased by a faceless man trying to kill him. Several times he had been at the top of a tall building or high bridge and pushed off. Just as he was about to hit the ground or the water, a large hand reached out and grabbed him, holding him until he climbed to safety. Then he was trapped in a burning building, unable to escape when, in the midst of the flames, he saw a face. It was the face of the sheriff, her hair burning the color of the fire. She reached out, took his hand in hers and led him safely outside where they stood arm in arm watching the building burn to the ground. He saw a large man running past, and it disturbed him that he couldn’t see his face. He chased the man, caught him and wrestled him to the ground. When he turned the man over, Jimbo stared up at him. Someone grabbed him from behind by the throat and when he turned to look it was “Bubba” choking him with his huge pine tar-stained hands. As he lost consciousness, he saw long tapered fingers grasping a gun, shouting to Bubba to let him go. Then he woke up.

He got out of bed and tried to remember where his uncle had told him the bathroom was. Stepping onto the tiled floor reminded him they still had no heat. There was a definite chill to the air, and the ceramic floor and porcelain plumbing fixtures caused him to shiver. It came as no surprise when he found cold water coming from both faucets. He finished as quickly as possible, wrapped the large towel from the back of the bathroom door around his shoulders and walked toward the sound of the television set. George sat in front of the TV, a hooded sweatshirt snugged about him, intently watching the weather channel, displaying the local and regional forecast for the next five days.

"It's as important as your fishing gear," his uncle said without looking away from the screen. "We don't want to be caught out on the water by a surprise storm. They can be pretty severe this time of year. The weather will dictate where we fish as well as how we fish. I always keep rain gear in the boat, the same as life jackets."

"What are they predicting for today?" Brad asked, trying to warm himself by rubbing his arms and legs. His uncle saw his antics and told him to dress in layers, as it tended to warm up quickly when the sun came out.

"Today's one of those percentage days," his uncle continued, still watching the screen. "They're expecting a cold front to come through, bringing some severe thunderstorms. The question is, when? It all depends on the speed it's traveling and that can vary widely. This could be a real blessing in disguise. The bass will tend to feed voraciously before an approaching front, and we could catch a lot of quality fish today. However, it may be of little help during the tournament, as the fish usually get lockjaw after the front moves through. Get yourself something to eat, and we'll hook up the old boat in the garage and meet Jimbo at the boat ramp."

Brad looked around the kitchen for anything suitable to eat that didn't need to be cooked. In one cabinet he found a box of dry cereal. It had been opened but it was about half full. He looked over the box, trying to find a freshness date or something to indicate how old the contents were. He decided against eating it, since he could find no bar code on the package. That would probably make the box at least five years old. On top of that, the milk carton in the refrigerator was three months out of date, and the contents looked brown and lumpy. He finally decided on a single-serving size can of baked beans he found in a cupboard. He located a can opener in a counter drawer among a variety of hand tools, old rubber bands and used plastic bag ties. In the sink, he found a plastic spoon, which he washed in cold water and dried on the towel from around his shoulders.

He cleared a space on the kitchen table cluttered with old newspapers, unopened junk mail, paper plates and cups. As he ate, he heard his uncle go out the door, start his pickup truck and back out from in front of the empty side of the garage and back into the side with his old bass boat. He came back into the house and asked Brad to help him line the trailer hitch up with the ball on his pickup bumper.

"I always keep this boat maintained and ready," George said. "I could have taken a brand-new boat, motor and trailer every year, but I prefer this one. Call it luck, call it superstition, but this was my first and it will be my last. The rig you saw at the garage by the factory is just for the tournament. You see, being the sponsor, they expect it. But when I fish otherwise, I use 'Old Faithful.' "

They hooked up the boat, plugged in the electrical connector, and George tried the turn signals, running lights and brake lights, and Brad acknowledged that they all worked. They made sure that the safety chains were attached and that the "break-away" cable for the emergency brake was hooked to the bumper.

George told him they each had five rod-and-reel combinations, with an appropriately-sized line for any conditions they were likely to encounter. He showed Brad five storage boxes containing every type of lure imaginable, hooks of every size and shape, a plethora of weights, swivels and ancillary items, such as glass beads and rattles.

"The manufacturers send me all this complimentary stuff, just so they can say they're used by a boat company, so don't be afraid to use any or all of it."

Brad's eyes widened like a kid in a candy shop. "There must be thousands of dollars worth of tackle here!"

"Probably more," George said. "Let's get going, Jimbo's going to be waiting. He's our guide today. While I've been up north, he's been keeping tabs on the fishing."

They pulled out of the driveway and headed back the way Brad had remembered them coming in yesterday, past the lovely stands of trees, past the half-hidden views of stained watered creek arms, past the decayed remains of rusted dreams and rotted hopes and past the sign leading them to the ashes of twenty years of his uncle's efforts. Someone, for some self-serving reason, was trying to take everything away from him including his life. Brad hoped that whoever it was, was willing to pay the price.

Brad's thoughts were interrupted as the pickup truck bounced over the rutted ground. His uncle turned around to get in position to back the boat into the water, the headlights playing over the remains of the factory like a light show at a rock concert. Brad saw a man come out of the garage carrying a bag in one hand. By the dim light of the first rays of the early morning sun, Brad recognized Jimbo walking toward them.

"Thought you boys might like some doughnuts and coffee before we hit the water," Jimbo said, as he set the bag down on the hood of Uncle George's truck and began to remove Styrofoam cups from it. Brad took one, letting the steam from the holes in the plastic lid warm his face as he selected a doughnut.

"Jimbo, you're a lifesaver!" Uncle George exclaimed while reaching for his breakfast.

They munched and drank, letting the hot liquid explore their chilled bodies, while Jimbo set about loosening the tie-downs and winch strap from the boat. He reached into a compartment and brought out the running and anchor lights, which he inserted into their respective receptacles, trying each in turn, saying, "We'll need to keep our lights on until the sun is high enough for us to be seen."

Jimbo walked around to the stem of the boat, checking to make sure the drain plug was tightly fitted in its hole. Finding it so, he pumped the bulb to ensure sufficient fuel to the engine. Jimbo climbed into the boat and put on a life jacket. He handed one to Brad and one to George, and the two men put theirs on. George got back into the truck while Brad walked down to the dock to wait for them to launch the boat. In one smooth motion, George backed the boat into the water. Jimbo started the engine as soon as the lower unit was far enough under, and proceeded to back the boat off the trailer, while George parked the truck and empty trailer and walked down to join his nephew on the boat dock. Jimbo drifted with a slight breeze as he waited for the engine to warm up and run smoothly, then shifting into forward, he idled over to the dock to pick up his passengers.

The smoke from the outboard motor mingled with the mist that blanketed the water, which was considerably warmer than the air. The "stick-ups" and "fall-downs" looked like an army of skeletal specters holding spears and swords as a threat to anyone brave enough to approach. Occasionally, over the sound of frogs croaking and insects buzzing, a fish could be heard slapping the surface as it chased a minnow or bug, hoping for an early morning meal. To Brad, it sounded like a symphony compared to the noise of horns honking and car engines racing. It was like a soothing balm on his troubled soul. His thoughts wandered. He thought about how all life had begun in the water, and it seemed natural to go back to it in his time of trouble. As they slowly pulled away from the dock, Brad saw streaks of sunlight paint strange patterns on the surface of the water and in the sky. He looked around, taking in the sights of their visible breath, the wake as the motor pushed them over the glassy surface of the water, and a "coot" paddling in small circles, stopping to dip its head under. Brad thought how great it was to be alive. Now, if they could just stay that way.

"We have to idle out of this creek, because what you see above the water is less than half of what's underneath," Jimbo commented causally, as they glided close to stumps and gently swaying tree trunks. "When we get to the mouth, we'll pick up a boat lane that will lead us to the main lake. You'll see the little fluorescent orange buoys about fifty yards apart, marking old river channels or road beds where we can run without worrying about stumps. The only thing we have to watch out for are floating logs that have fallen off, or been knocked or blown off the flooded trees."

The ride to the main lake was a new and exciting experience for Brad, like his first automobile trip. The buoys marked the middle of the channel, so they were safe as long as they stayed within a boat's width on either side. As they raced from marker to marker at forty to fifty miles per hour, it reminded Brad of driving down a twisting tree-lined road. He was exhilarated, his hair blowing wildly with the wind they were generating from the speed of the boat. Occasionally, they came upon another boat coming toward them on the other side of the buoys, which they passed with a slight rocking motion and a mist of spray from the rooster tail of the other boat. Looking back, he could see the waves from their passing spreading out farther and wider, causing the bare branches of the flooded trees to swing to and fro, as if blown by a selective wind.

"We're heading for a large shallow area with humps," yelled Jimbo against the noise of the wind. "It's covered with grass, and the bass should be spawning. We'll drift from hump to hump, ripping a 'rattle trap,' through the tops of the grass, or pull a Carolina rig plastic lizard along the tops of the ridges and see if we can get bit. Some pre-spawn bass should be cruising the humps looking for a quick snack."

They left the small orange markers behind, motoring into the large red and green buoys of the main lake boat lane. The distance between the buoys was over twice the width of their boat, so two boats could safely run side by side or pass one another without worrying about submerged timber. George leaned close to Brad so he could talk without having to shout, and told him the red and green buoys were so arranged as to indicate the direction one was heading toward or away from the dam. The north-south boat lane they were running in was on the Louisiana side and fairly close to the shore, which consisted of low clay and sandy bluffs, deeply undercut by the action of the waves. From time to time, a tree was leaning out into the water, its roots no longer able to hold it up in the washed out soil. Along other areas, trees that once lined the old river channel were standing well out in the water, leaves no longer emerging from the long-dead branches. Brad saw points formed by coves that opened the bluffwall. Some of the coves were no larger than small bays, others went so far back that they looked like other lakes. Brad had never run at such a high speed for so long without reaching the end or going in circles on other bodies of water. They made a long, wide sweeping "S" curve, then Jimbo backed off on the throttle as they approached a large area bounded by shoreline on the west, a one-mile line of flooded trees about a mile to the north, and ending at a north-south boat lane that connected the one they had come in. Jimbo climbed to the forward casting deck, lowered the trolling motor, switched on the fish locater, and began to move the boat into the wind. George leaned against the rear "butt seat," readying his rod for the first cast. "Brad, get up there with Jimbo and fish back-to-back with him," George said, pointing with his rod tip. "He'll explain to you how and why we're fishing here."

"The bass use these ridges and humps like highways from the shoreline to deep water," Jimbo explained once Brad got comfortable. "The grass gives them security, plus an ambush point if they see an opportunity for a meal. The ridges are from eighteen to twenty feet deep, and the humps about eight to ten, so we'll try to drift along a hump by watching the depth on our locater We'll try casting a Carolina rigged, cotton candy-colored plastic lizard and pull it through the grass. Meanwhile, one of us can try throwing a rattle trap and just rip it over the top of the grass. If we don't get bit here, we'll try some main lake points. You see, we're trying to establish a pattern, if we can. We'll try it again tomorrow, and if it holds, you can try it during the tournament."

On his first cast, Brad used the Carolina rig. He was having trouble feeling the difference between a bite and the grass pulling on his weight, and he said as much to George.

"Don't be in too much of a hurry," his uncle replied. "Lift the rod tip straight up until the weight comes off the bottom, then if you've got a fish, you'll feel it and you can set the hook."

As he finished saying that, George lowered his rod tip, tightening the line, until it was parallel to the water. He then set the hook with a violent, upward pull of his arms. The rod tip stayed down, pulsing with rhythmic action, while the rod bent from the weight of the fish and the pressure of his pull. The seasoned fisherman pumped and wound, pumped and wound, occasionally lowering the rod to keep the fish from jumping and possibly throwing the hook from its jaw. Finally, giving up its struggle, the fish came up as George bent to one knee. He reached over the side and "lipped" the fish, lifting it up and into the boat.

"Nice fish, Unc," cheered Brad, hardly able to control his excitement. "Looks like a three- or four-pounder."

George proceeded to remove the hook from the bass's lower jaw, held it by the lip and supported the tail, giving Jimbo and Brad a good look at the first bass of the day. Its back was dark green with black splotches along its lateral line. The belly was white and heavy with spawn. Brad had never seen colors as dark on a largemouth bass.

"The bass gets its dark colors from spending a lot of time in the thick grass," Jimbo informed Brad. "It's a good sign that these fish have been in here for quite a while. I'd say she was on her way to the shoreline to spawn."

Carefully, Uncle George lowered the bass into the water, moving it forward and back, forcing water through it's gills to revive it, he released his hold and watched as it swam away. On the upward sweep of his rod, Brad felt a slight "tick" and saw the line jump. He stopped his movement with the rod straight up. He watched the line hanging limp from the tip of the rod to where it disappeared into the water. Suddenly, it began to jump and move off to the right. Brad turned the handle of his reel, taking the slack from the line while lowering his rod. Then, he reared back and set the hook with a mighty effort.

"That's what we came here for!" Brad howled, cranking the reel and raising and lowering the rod. In his excitement, he reeled the bass clear up out of the water, nearly hitting Jimbo in the back of the head with it as he swung the rod around. With the three of them laughing, the fish almost landed back in the water as it unhooked itself and fell to the bottom of the boat. Brad scrambled around, trying to grab the bass as it flopped about, disgorging small bait fish. Finally, he was able to lip the bass and, figuring it had suffered enough, returned it to the water. It jumped and splashed and swam away, apparently none the worse for wear. Jimbo laughed and said that it liked Brad so well, it was trying to jump back into the boat.

And so it went. When they had drifted almost into the line of trees and stumps, they restarted the big motor, putt-putted back to where they had begun, and resumed fishing.

They were doing so well, they hardly noticed the wind beginning to pick up. Brad was the first to comment on the dark clouds that suddenly appeared overhead. Before they had a chance to do anything, the first flash of lightning, followed immediately by a clap of thunder, told them they had waited too long. As if a gigantic hand had pushed them, they were propelled sideways into the stump field and held by the force of the wind against a tree. Jimbo's hat was plucked from his head and it disappeared as a rain squall overtook them. Things were made worse by the waves, which were beginning to wash against the gunwale of the boat. They were afraid of being swamped as the waves, driven by the sudden wind, got higher and higher.

"Let's get the hell out of here!" Jimbo yelled above the shrieking wind and rumbling thunder. They all made sure their life jackets were securely fastened while Jimbo tried to start the big engine. The challenge now was backing out and away from the trees without taking too much water over the stern of the boat. Trying to go forward would only succeed in driving them deeper into the stump field, and increase the chances of the wildly pitching boat being impaled upon a submerged stump. Luck and the powerful engine enabled them to back up enough for the wind to help turn them in the right direction long enough to gain forward momentum. The peaceful water had become large white-capped rollers that broke over the bow of the boat. By proceeding slowly and trying to meet the waves at a forty-five-degree angle, they were able to reach the boat lane. However, when they started into the curve, they found they were no longer protected by the shoreline, and the waves coming at them were twice as high. First, the bow of the boat pointed toward the black sky, Then it plummeted down, as if it were heading straight for the bottom, when at the last minute, it popped up with water streaming over the casting deck, soaking the three from head to foot as the torrential rain beat down upon them. The water they were taking on activated the bilge pump automatically, and for the time being, it was keeping them from being swamped.

"We've got to get out of these waves!" Jimbo screamed. "Got to get to a cove!"

There were lots of coves as they had seen on their way

out. The problem was going to be the right turn required to get into one, which, unless Jimbo's seamanship was flawless, would mean taking the waves directly from the side. At best, they would be swamped. At worst, they would be flipped over sideways, or "rolled onto their beam ends." The timing had to be precise. Jimbo had to match the speed of the boat to the speed of the oncoming wave, so they would turn into and stay in the trough of the wave, riding it until they entered the cove. With a shout that was lost in the noise of the storm, a stab of the throttle and a hard turn of the steering wheel, Jimbo shot for the cove.

Reaching the entrance was like coming to the end of an amusement park water ride. He backed off the throttle, and with only a jet of water issuing from the bilge pump discharge to remind them of what they had come through, Jimbo glided slowly to the back of the cove, running the bow of the boat up on the muddy shore. There was a boat dock of sorts. Its weather-beaten pilings were half-rotten, slats were broken and missing, but it was occupied by several boats. Brad jumped off, grabbed the bow line, secured it around a convenient tree, while Jimbo and George, already soaked to the skin, walked up the path and into the building which proudly advertised "Bar and Restaurant." Brad squeezed some of the water from his hat, pushed back his wet hair and followed them in.

As overcast as it was outside, it was darker still inside. At first glance, Brad affirmed it was a rectangular room slightly narrower on the inside than on the outside. He concluded the missing space must be occupied by the kitchen and restroom. The outside walls were set with wooden booths that looked homemade or at least home-repaired. The middle of the room was arranged with round tables which looked like old folding card tables, with chairs that didn't match. The inside wall sported long benches, presumably for larger parties, which looked like old picnic tables no longer usable by the forest preserves. The only light came from electric faux candles in the booths, and the jukebox in the corner, which was blaring an outdated country-western tune. Behind the small bar, at the narrow end of the room hung two old beer signs, but only one was half lit. No bottles or mirrors were to be seen, which meant either they didn't have any or they were kept out of the customers' easy reach, so they couldn't be used as projectiles. Adding to Brad's uneasy feeling was the fact that he could smell the little deodorizer cake in the urinals from the front door. This seemed consistent with the overall decor of the place, which included dusty cobwebs hanging from the ceiling and muddy sand on the floor. Brad couldn't speak for Jimbo or his uncle, but his appetite suddenly disappeared.

About twelve men sat at two of the old picnic tables, and by the pile of empty beer cans lying about, they looked as if they were trying to drink Milwaukee dry. Jimbo suggested they sit at a round table as far away from the others as possible. They stood for a few minutes peeling off as much wet clothing as decency allowed. Hanging these on the backs of their chairs, they sat down. At the bar, Brad saw a gray-haired bearded man. Every now and then, the old man reached down to pet his dog, who lay at his feet chewing what looked like a bone of some sort. From the door which must have been the kitchen, a woman entered.

In the dim light, Brad caught sight of the shapeliest figure in short shorts and high heels, this side of Hollywood She moved across the room like she was walking down the runway at the Miss America contest, and from what Brad saw, she would have been the winner. He couldn't take his eyes from her body. Her bare legs were flawless. Her derriere looked like two bear cubs wrestling in a sack as she walked, and her chest would have rivaled Dolly Parton. She wore a manly shirt tied above her tiny waist, the buttons straining to contain its contents.

"What'll you have, fellas'?" she purred as she leaned on the table, supporting herself with her hands. The pressure against the sides of her chest with that maneuver made Brad gasp and shift his gaze in embarrassment.

At first, he thought it was a sick joke. In the poor light, she seemed to be wearing a prize-winning Halloween mask Brad thought, what a cruel trick of nature to place one of the ugliest faces he had ever seen atop one of the hottest bodies. Her complexion was horrid, and her features were coarse, almost masculine. Their proportions were all wrong. A "bad hair day" might have been an improvement to her mess of a mane. Little wonder she worked in a place like this, Brad thought. She might even have owned the place, as he doubted if she would have been hired.

"Three beers, Dolly," Uncle George said, forcing a smile while looking at her. As she walked away, he shook his head sadly and said, "What a waste!"

"Dolly?" Brad exclaimed. "You've got to be kidding! It's too ironic for words."

"Don't kid yourself," Jimbo chimed in. "That song 'The Girls All Get Prettier At Closing Time,' goes a long way in here. On the weekends, her dance card reads like the local telephone book."

Dolly came back with the beers and set them down on the table. She picked up the money George had taken out of his damp wallet, and he told her to keep the change. She brushed herself slowly against Brad's shoulder as she turned to walk away. Stopping to apologize, Dolly made sure he saw the exaggerated wink she shot him. The effort wasn't lost on him, as he flushed deeply. It wasn't lost on the group at the other table, either.

The music stopped, and loud grumbling from the far end of the room drifted to their ears. Brad and the others knew they were being sized up, and they didn't much like the odds. George suggested they leave, but before they could gather their damp clothes, six of the men from across the room walked over to stand between them and the door. Another six came over and stood, forming a semicircle around them. As Brad suspected, every mob had a leader, and this group was no different.

"You think you can just walk in here and have your way with our women?" the leader asked, stepping up into Brad's face. Now, Brad knew that the man's animosity had nothing to do with Dolly. It probably had a lot to do with him being a stranger and just as much to do with the men being drunk. And maybe, Brad sensed, something more.

"And whom do I have the pleasure of addressing?" Brad asked in his most collegiate voice.

"Well, professor," the man slurred, "the name's Tucker, Tucker Jones. Not that it makes any difference to you!"

"Let's just calm down here," Jimbo interjected as he stepped between Brad and Tucker Jones. "There's no cause for hard feelings. Let us buy you boys a beer."

Tucker squinted his rheumy eyes, and focused on Jimbo's face. Then he took a step back, hooked his thumbs in the straps of his bib overalls and looked him up and down.

"Hey, I know you! You're the foreman of that there boat company," Tucker slurred. "Yeah, people like you and that boss of yours come down here and hire cheap labor, buy cheap land and build classy boats that nobody around here can afford to buy. That place shoulda been blown up years ago."

That was enough for George. He forced his way into their midst, and grabbed Tucker by his straps. With their faces inches apart, he said, "What do you mean 'blown up,' you no-account troublemaker?"

"Did he say 'blown up'?" Brad asked.

Suddenly, a chair came flying over and hit George on the back of his head and neck, causing him to slump to the floor without a sound. In the dim light, Brad couldn't see who was responsible for the deed, but that started the ball rolling. Jimbo quickly bent over to protect George from further injury as several men dove on him. Brad grabbed Tucker, spun him around and with a strangle hold, used him as a shield against attacks from the front. As Brad had learned in Barroom Brawling 101, the safest place to be is with one's back to a wall or, if no wall is available, back-to-back with someone you trust. Sensing the same thing, Jimbo heaved George over his shoulder like a bag of sand and stood upright among the flying bodies. Then, holding George with one hand, he picked up a table by one leg and used it like a battering ram, cleared a path to the corner by the kitchen.

Brad followed him, still clutching Tucker. Even in the dim light, Brad could see that he had turned a nice shade of blue. One of the men rushed at him from behind and grabbed his left shoulder. Brad leaned forward, putting his weight on the limp body of Tucker. kicked back with his left foot, hitting the shin of his attacker. He heard the unseen man hit the floor, wailing in pain. When he got to the corner, Brad dropped the limp body to the floor.

Breathing hard, he said to Jimbo, "Put Uncle George down, and we'll stack the bad guys in front so they'll have to climb over their own to get at us."

With that, they were a well oiled machine: Jimbo would reach out and grab a man with one hand, hit him with the other and drop him on the growing pile. Brad had torn a leg from the table Jimbo had dropped, and was using it like a club, taking a terrible toll.

As quickly as it started, it was over. Brad and Jimbo were standing shoulder-to-shoulder in the corner, fire still blazing in their eyes, the madness of battle still coursing through their veins. Before them lay twelve bodies, some moaning, others trying to crawl away, and some not moving at all. Now was the time for them to see to their own wounds, as they had felt none of the punches or objects thrown at them. It was also the time to see to Uncle George, who was sitting up, holding his head and rocking back and forth.

The front door opened. Pat and four of her deputies walked in, nightsticks ready. After her eyes adjusted to the dim light, Pat stepped over broken tables, sprawled bodies and empty beer cans, on her way to where Brad and Jimbo were trying to lift Uncle George slowly to his feet and find him an unbroken chair to sit on.

"George? Brad? Is that you?" she asked. "What the hell's going on here? Dolly called and said the local boys were about to kill three strangers. If you're the three strangers, you don't look dead. But some of them others ain't looking too healthy. Jimbo, you take George and go with one of my deputies to the hospital. Brad, you better come down to my office with me and tell me all about this. I have a feeling this is more than just a drunken brawl."

"Do me one favor, please," Brad said. "Bring Tucker Jones with us. I think he knows something about what's been going on with Uncle George."

Pat agreed. "I can hold him for twenty-four hours on disorderly conduct, unless you can convince me he's more than just a drunken troublemaker."

Brad got into the front seat of the squad car, and waited for Pat to finish giving instructions to her deputies about taking statements from Dolly and anybody else who wasn't going to the hospital. He thought he saw Pat walking toward the car, but coming around to the passenger side was Dolly.

The barmaid came up to the open window, put her slim hand in, touching a trickle of blood drying behind Brad's ear and cooed, "Come back later, handsome, and I'll make all those nasty bruises feel better." Then she pivoted on one shapely leg, and strolled seductively back into the bar. Brad followed her movements, shaking his head and thinking to himself that natural light didn't help her a bit. Suddenly, he realized the storm had passed and the sun was shining.

"Quite a view from this angle," Pat said, looking past Brad, following Dolly's progress up the path. "You forget something?"

"Nope," Brad said, turning his head to look into Pat's eyes. "Not a thing."

Pat got behind the wheel, fastened her seat belt, and started the engine. Putting the car into gear, she started down the road to Hemphill.

"Dolly said she'd guard your uncle's boat with her life. She'll tie it up to the dock good and proper when the good ol' boys are gone," Pat said curtly. Brad didn't answer, as he had heard that tone of voice before. Although he didn't understand her reasons, he knew jealousy when he heard it.

"Dolly lives in a trailer behind the bar, so it'll be safe

enough. You can get it in the morning . . . or tonight, if you prefer.

Again, Brad didn't answer. The sheriff pulled off the side of the road and turned to face him.

"Look!" she started to say, a hard edge to her voice. Brad slowly turned to her, and Pat's voice softened as she saw his face. "Brad, you're hurt! All those bruises and cuts. Oh, your poor beautiful face." Tears welled up in her eyes as she gently cradled his head to her bosom and began to whisper as a mother soothes an injured child.

Brad was torn apart. He didn't want to move his head from its heavenly pillow, but her badge was branding his cheek. There was only one thing he could do. He pulled his head away and seeing the hurt look in her eyes, took her by the shoulders, pulled her to him, put his lips to hers and kissed her long and hard. She parted her soft lips in response to his pressure, wrapping her strong arms around his neck. He could have winced from the pain of his bruises, but instead, rose to the passion of her embrace. No words were needed as they slipped into the back seat, shedding useless clothing as they went. Then she was over him, rough and demanding at first, then becoming soft and responsive.

Later, their passion spent, their breathing returning to normal but not ready yet for words, they got out of the back, and returned to the front seat. They both knew that they couldn't just drive away as if nothing had happened, yet neither felt guilty nor one bit apologetic.

Brad was the first to speak. "Nothing like this has ever happened to me before."

"If that's an apology," she exhaled, "please don't. I would have taken you the first time I met you if your uncle hadn't been there. I don't blame Dolly. I never met anyone who oozed sexuality more than you."

"I hope it meant more to you than that," Brad sighed.

"Just enjoy it, kid. I did. It was just physical," she lied.

"God, you're hard! I refuse to believe that's all it was to you. You make me feel dirty, like a . . . like a . . ." He couldn't even say the word. This couldn't be happening to him. It was all turned around; men were supposed to act like that, not women.

When they got to the station, Uncle George and Jimbo were already there, sitting at a desk, filling out papers of some sort. There was no sign of Tucker Jones or the others. Brad walked in, tucking his shirt into his pants and adjusting his belt, followed by Pat, buttoning the last few top buttons of her shirt and adjusting her gun-belt and support strap.

Uncle George gave Brad a knowing look, but Brad just shook his head, took an empty chair and rested his chin on his hands. He was completely confused. Pat wasn't the kind of girl he was normally attracted to. But what happened between them, he was sure, was more than physical. As to her reaction, it not only didn't make sense, it didn't do much for his libido. He made a mental note: the next time he saw her, he would look at her gun and see if there were any notches on its grip.

Brad reflected on the events of the day. They found and caught enough bass to do well in the tournament, if the pattern held. It was one of the best days fishing he had ever experienced. He had endured the worst storm on the water he had ever seen or heard about. He had seen the most beautiful and the ugliest woman in his life, and she was the same person. He was in the dirtiest bar, the worst fight and had the best sex all in the same afternoon. All things considered, it was the best day he ever had. Life was good, he thought. A smile tried to break out on his face but one of his bruises stopped it, leaving a kind of smirk. Pat observed this curiously as she sat down across the desk from him.

"What's this about Tucker Jones having something to do with the attempts on George's life?" she asked.

"When I walked around the burned-out factory," Brad explained, "there was one area in particular that looked as if an explosion blew the debris out in all directions from a central point. I couldn't find anything that would have caused that to happen if it was a simple fire. But at the bar, before the fight started, Tucker came over to our table and said somebody should have blown the place up before. He had obviously been drinking and his tongue was well lubricated. After he said it, he looked and sounded like he put his foot in his mouth, but before I could find out if it was just coincidental, Uncle George was blindsided by a chair. And the rest, as they say, is history."

"It could be something, or it could be nothing," Pat concluded. "But why Tucker? He hardly knows your uncle." She seemed to be talking to Brad, but she was really thinking out loud. As if finally making up her mind, she said, "Tell you what I'm going to do. Those bomb people came up this morning and picked up that thing you found in your uncle's truck. By the way, you were a hundred percent right about what it was and how it worked. That's why I'm going along with you on this. They left me a kit which I can use to tell whether a person has handled explosives or incendiary devices recently. It makes no difference if they wash their hands, it will still show. I'm going to use it on Tucker. I doubt if he was smart enough to use gloves, and if he tests positive, maybe I can get him to talk. Meanwhile, you and your uncle try to stay out of trouble. I'll have enough of a time trying to explain why I'm holding Tucker and some of his friends, but not you boys. Now, I'll have one of my deputies run you up to your truck."

Brad thanked her, gathered Jimbo and his uncle and followed the deputy out the back door to the waiting squad car. George told the deputy where they had left his pickup as they turned out of the parking lot.

George leaned forward and tapped their driver on the shoulder. "Say deputy, could you make a quick stop at the bank as long as we're in town? I'd like to cash a check. They'll be closed by the time we could get back here in my truck."

"I'm not really supposed to . . . well, okay, but make it fast," the deputy said as he hit the brake and turned into the bank parking lot.

"Come in with me, Brad," George said. "I'm not too steady yet."

They got out of the squad car and walked into the bank as George reached into a pocket inside his jacket and removed a plastic "zipper" type bag, from which he extracted a check book and his wallet.

"Keeps them dry," he remarked casually as they walked to a teller's window. He was about to explain to the girl behind the cage what he wanted, when a man came out of a side office and approached them. He was tall, slim and well-dressed in what Brad thought was an awfully nice suit for what he had seen so far of this town. He reached out a smooth hand with long fingers ending in manicured nails.

"Hello, George," he said in a practiced, oily voice. "This is so opportune. I was going to come out to see you. That corporation we represent upped their offer for your company."

"How nice," Uncle George responded, sarcastically. "You must be the only one in town who doesn't know my factory burned to the ground yesterday."

"I knew that," he replied, "but they are still interested in your designs and, of course, the property."

"Then you're talking to the wrong person. Reed Hadley, meet Brad Allen, my nephew. He owns the land the factory sat on."

In unison, Reed Hadley and Brad said "What?!"

"Now, if you'll excuse me, I'd like to cash a check. We're in a hurry," Uncle George said, as he turned back to the teller. He wrote out the check for cash, counted the money he received and walked out of the door. Reed Hadley stood there, a strained look on his face as if he had just flatulated, while Brad followed his uncle out. Brad turned his head, first back to Mr. Hadley, then to his uncle, and he almost ran into the door.

Back in the squad car, Brad asked, "What just happened in there?"

"You remember," his uncle replied. "I told you before larger corporations have made offers to buy my company. They usually present their offers through bank officers like Hadley. He's the president of this bank. I never liked him. He reminds me of my ex-brother-in-law. Thinks his shit doesn't stink."

"Not that," Brad countered, "The part about him talking to the wrong person. What did you mean when you said I owned the land?"

"Your father never told you? You didn't read it in his will?" his uncle queried.

"No, my father never told me, and I haven't had time to read the will. Maybe you can enlighten me."

"Let me start at the beginning," Uncle George began. "Twenty years ago, when I first decided to move here and go into the boat business, your father lent me the money to purchase the land, as I didn't have enough to cover what the building and supplies cost. Your father was a better businessman than I am, and figured if I went belly up, he could get his money back for the land, maybe even make a profit if property values increased. Well, over the years, the subject never came up. Oh, I could have paid your father back with interest, but that wasn't his style. He knew I was doing well, but so was his investment, and he didn't need the money. He always said when I retire and sell out, he would use the money in his old age or leave it to you. It didn't work out the way either one of us planned, but the land is yours. Maybe I'm too old to rebuild. I was hoping you would come into the business and take over when I retired, since it's half yours anyway. That's why this week is going to be important to me, too. It will give me time to think."

No one spoke for a long time, then Uncle George resumed. "Jimbo, I feel bad for you. You've been with me a long time I won't know what to do without you."

"Boss, remember a long time ago, you trusted me when I needed your help? I told you I'd stay with you as long as you needed me. Well, the way I see it, you still need me. I don't live a very extravagant lifestyle and I don't need money. If you don't rebuild the factory, you'll still need a fishing buddy."

George's eyes clouded up, Brad sniffed noisily, and the deputy driving the squad car stared straight ahead, dabbing ineffectively at his eyes.

Arriving at the remains of the boat factory, they said goodbye to Jimbo and watched him as he backed his old pickup truck from the garage and headed off down the road. Uncle George, looking at his watch, suggested that they drive to the bar and retrieve the boat.

"We have enough daylight left for me to bring the boat back, while you can drive the truck back here. One thing we don't do around here is night fishing. Too dangerous. Even the old timers won't run the lake after dark. Jimbo has told me of several of the locals, not paying attention to the time, having to tie up to a stump and spend the night sleeping on the deck of their boat, rather than risk 'running' in the dark. We can leave the boat tied to the dock here and be on the water at first light, instead of having to get it tomorrow."

Brad agreed, although he wasn't thrilled at the prospect of seeing Dolly again. He hoped they could get the boat and leave without being seen. He wasn't good at confrontations, and from the way she looked at him earlier and the things she'd said, he knew he'd either have to fish or cut bait.

It didn't take them long to get to the bar. Brad paid particular attention to the route his uncle took, so that he would be able to find his way back. There were other pickup trucks parked in front, plus a few old cars. Uncle George went around the building toward the boat dock, telling Brad he had no daylight to burn.

"Go in and tell Dolly I'm taking the boat, and thank her for keeping an eye on it," he said over his shoulder. "I'll see you back at the factory."

Brad stood in front of the door, searching his mind for some excuse to prevent him from going in. Several times he reached out for the door handle, but each time he withdrew his hand. Just then, the door opened and two men walked out, stopping abruptly to avoid bumping into Brad. They paused just long enough for their eyes to adjust to the fading sunlight, focused with some difficulty on Brad's face, smiled indifferently, and got into one of the trucks. Shrugging his shoulders, Brad stepped through the open door. Someone had taken the time to rearrange the tables and chairs, and Brad marveled at the repairs to the broken and damaged items. He thought that perhaps the repairs were routine, and the speed and expertise came from experience. As the door closed behind him, shutting out the light, everything looked as though no fight had taken place.

Walking to the bar, he noticed the same man sitting there with the same dog at his feet. Then again, he thought, it could have been another man or another dog. But as he saw a figure emerge from the kitchen door, there was no mistaking Dolly. The shadows and dim light, as before, were good to her and suddenly Brad no longer dreaded their meeting. He pitied her, and that gave him strength.

"Hello, Handsome. So you decided to take me up on my offer of first aid?" Dolly purred as she hooked her arm through his.

"Actually," Brad replied, "I just came in to thank you for watching my uncle's boat and that he's taking it back to his dock so we can be on the water at first light." Brad could feel the pressure of her fullness against his arm as she tried to pull him closer. "I also wanted to apologize for any damage we may have caused, but the sheriff's holding the fellas who s-started it," he stuttered, feeling her warm breath against his neck. "I really have to be getting along. I've got to pick up my uncle, and we're supposed to see the sheriff tonight," Brad lied.

"Go see the sheriff, then!" she snapped, releasing his arm and pushing him away. "See if you can get anything off of that tight-assed bitch!" As she walked away, she thought to herself if anybody could, it would be him. Relieved, Brad found his way outside, got back into his uncle's truck and retraced the route back to the burned-out factory.

Uncle George was already there when Brad pulled

onto the path leading to the boat ramp. In the light from the headlamps, he could see the police insignia glowing on the side of the car as his uncle and the sheriff leaned against it. Across the creek, the orange ball of the sun was just disappearing, leaving a wash of colors staining the sky and water. He couldn't help but notice the outline of the sheriff's silhouette and the shadow it cast on the light-colored squad-car. He immediately thought of the last time he was in the car with her, and felt glad it was too dark for anyone to see the sudden flush of color he was sure had come over his face.

"This is a pleasant surprise," Brad commented to Pat as he walked over to join in their conversation, hoping the still evening and beautiful sunset would soften her heart. He refused to believe that she could dismiss their afternoon lovemaking as just another form of physical exercise.

"I came over to tell you the results of the test I performed on Tucker Jones," she explained matter-of-factly. "It was positive. He had definitely handled explosives recently."

"I knew it!" Brad exclaimed. "You can charge him with blowing up the factory and there's a good chance he made the bomb we found in the truck."

"As I was just telling your Uncle George," Pat continued in her even tone, "Tucker claims he was using dynamite to blow up some stumps. Some of his friends are willing to testify to that effect if we try to press charges. I think he's lying about the stumps, but we haven't any evidence or witnesses to the contrary. I also don't think he's smart enough to have done the car bomb. But the worst part is trying to come up with a motive. I'll agree he's no choirboy, but other than being drunk and disorderly, he has no serious priors. I'm going to hold him until I talk to

Dolly and see if she wants to make him pay damages, but after that, I'm going to have to let him go."

"Well, we're right about where we started," George said sadly, shaking his head.

"That's not true," Brad said, trying to cheer him up. "We have a pretty good idea of what pattern the bass are on."

"And I thought you were a fisherman," George snickered. "After that stormfront that went through here this afternoon, we'll be lucky to see a bass on the humps."

"I don't believe you guys!" Pat broke in. "Your business gets burned to the ground, someone's trying to kill you, you nearly get your head busted in a bar fight, and all you can talk about is bass fishing. What is it about fishing that's so all-fired great?"

"Well," Brad said, winking at his uncle, "you know how after you've been fishing all day, catching lots of bass and lipping them, kissing them and releasing them, then you open a package of kippered beef jerky and the salt stings your raw thumb, you eat it down to the last bite and as you put the final piece in your mouth, it smells and tastes like raw fish? It just doesn't get any better than that!"

George and Brad looked at each other, and in the light of the truck's headlamps, Pat could see by the knowing smiles on their faces that fishing was indeed life for them, and all the rest was just details. It wasn't that she disliked fishing. Quite the contrary, she fancied herself a pretty fair bass fisher, but to her it was a matter of priorities. Their method of prioritizing must have been a "man thing," she concluded.

"What you need is a motive," Pat said, as she walked around the front of the squad car and opened the driver's door. "What you need is some evidence. What you need is a witness. What you have is fishing on your minds, when it's your asses you should be worrying about!" With that, she started the engine and with a great show of spinning her tires, raced down the gravel path, turned onto the road and was gone, leaving Brad and his uncle standing in the glare of the lights of the pickup truck.

"I think she really likes you," Uncle George said. "Yessir, I really think she does."

4

Brad was about to respond when he realized they hadn't eaten since the coffee and doughnuts Jimbo brought in the morning, and he was voraciously hungry. Getting back in the truck, they were soon heading for a quiet place that served good food and plenty of it.

The billboard read "Lakeside Supper Club." Among other things, it advertised "Good Food," and at the bottom corner, a neon light spelled out "OPEN." The crowded parking lot told Brad that either they actually had good food or it was the only place open.

"You're too much of a pessimist," Uncle George exclaimed. "You can't judge every place around here by Dolly's."

The entrance to the restaurant was made to look like a boarding ramp on a cruise ship and, as Brad expected, the decor was nautical and the fare was a delightful combination of seafood and Cajun specialties. Brad decided on the buffet, which offered a taste of everything, and George ordered the catch of the day, which wasn't bass and the salmon certainly wasn't caught that day, at least not around there. They both ordered beers, and Brad was pleasantly surprised to find that each came in a frosty mug instead of a can that he had to open himself. They both applied themselves to eating, and it wasn't until after several trips back to the buffet for Brad before either felt like talking.

"What did you mean when you said we would be lucky to see a bass on the humps tomorrow?" Brad asked.

"I'd expect after today's storm front, tomorrow we'll have a high 'bluebird' sky. That usually pulls the bass deep, or causes them to suspend. Sometimes, they just tuck their noses into the grass and you'd have to hit them on the head with your lure to get them to even look at it. In any case, we'll try some main lake points and if nothing else works, boat docks. Some of the fish that stayed back in the creeks may not have been affected by the storm, and may be catchable. The bottom line is, whether or not the fishing is good, I don't think they'll be on the same pattern. Whatever we find, probably won't hold for the tournament. The good news is, the weather has been the same for everyone and it may end up being just luck or chance that wins."

Their appetites satisfied, they sat sipping slowly on the warm dregs at the bottom of the once-frosty mugs. Brad cast his gaze around the room. He was a thousand miles from home, at a restaurant between two small towns whose total population was less than the enrollment of the last college he attended. For some unexplainable reason, he expected the people to look and act quite differently from those in his neighborhood. The ones he observed in this supper club looked and acted no different than people at home. His uncle was right: it was wrong for him to judge everyone by what he had seen and done at Dolly's Bar. At that moment, he had a vision of himself leaning back in his chair, thumbs hooked in wide suspenders, a long black cigar held loosely in his teeth, all his physical needs attended to, at peace with the world. Thrusting these thoughts from his mind, he realized the day's activities had drained him. If he was going to be able to concentrate on fishing and helping his uncle with his problems, not to mention stay alive, what he needed now was sleep. George was nodding contentedly, so without a word, they got up, paid the bill and started for George's house.

It seemed to Brad like he had just put his head down on the pillow when his uncle shook him back to consciousness. A toothbrush working back and forth in his mouth, George muttered something about getting to the boat dock, not keeping Jimbo waiting, and a few other things lost in the rinsing and spitting. As his uncle had promised, the early morning sky was crystal clear. The stars shone like diamonds, and just a hint of sunlight was beginning to show on the eastern horizon. The air was a dead calm, heavy with humidity but without a hint of a breeze. Tiny insects buzzed incessantly around the yard light, trying to get in to sacrifice their lives to the heat of the bulb. The dew was running down the windshield and hood of the pickup truck as they prepared to leave for the boat ramp.

As usual, Jimbo was ready to go, with coffee and doughnuts to break their morning fast. Brad was tempted to ask Jimbo if he ever slept, but thought better of it, deciding the man's simple loyalty and dedication to his friend and employer was too sacred to demean with such a mundane question. Instead, he greeted the big man warmly and thanked him for his thoughtfulness in supplying the morning meal as the hot coffee explored his insides.

The look on Jimbo's face revealed his satisfaction, as he had taken quite a liking to George's nephew and did his best to please him. Jimbo had a keen sense of when people were treating him like a big, dumb puppy, and he felt this hurt more intensely than any physical blow. He'd never felt the need to go to great lengths to impress others with his wit or wisdom and it was a select few like

George Allen and Brad Allen, who had the ability to look past the callused, weather-beaten exterior to see the soul of a sensitive, intelligent and fiercely loyal man. The locals found him uncomplicated, unassuming and charming, and took to him, readily sharing their fishing knowledge and secrets. Local bullies or hard cases found him a formidable enemy, and left him alone.

The boat seats glistened with dew as Jimbo got in and started the engine, which coughed to life, smoked and sputtered for a few minutes, then smoothed out into a consistent idle. Little wonder, Brad thought, that the E.P.A. looked with a jaundiced eye at the two-cycle engine manufacturers and their big, gas-thirsty, oil-burning motors. It was the same old story: a multibillion-dollar a year recreational fishing and boating industry versus the environmentalists. There were those who for the sake of clean air and water would give up their jobs, their homes and take food from their babies' mouths. But while Brad had always seen things as either black or white, his father had often reminded him that as he grew in experience and maturity, he would begin to see some issues in various shades of gray. Brad thought life was getting more complicated; he must have been getting old.

"Don't stand there daydreaming, Brad. Get in the boat," his uncle shouted above the sound of the engine. George was already seated, and holding the dock to prevent them from drifting away.

They idled away from the dock, slowly coming to the first markers indicating the middle of the channel and safe water. In the first rays of the early morning sun, the calm water and fluorescent buoys looked like a smooth paved blacktop with only little cat's paws in a trail behind the boat. Several times along the way, they pulled out of the boat lane and idled through a stump field, watching the water temperature and depth sounder. Jimbo explained that if they were going to find any aggressive bass, they would have to find warm water about ten to fifteen feet deep. They ended up working their way along a lee shoreline, holding the boat back so that they were casting into ten feet of water. Brad and George were using Carolina-rigged wrinkle-cut pieces of soft plastic called "French fries," while Jimbo tried casting a black rattle jig with a plastic frog trailer, letting it settle to the bottom, then "hopping" it slowly back to the boat. On his second cast, Brad threw close to a small bush just above the surface of the water. As the heavy weight dragged the lure down, he felt the line go limp, then he noticed it began to move slowly against the current. Taking up the slack in the line while lowering the rod tip, he reared back and set the hook.

Feeling the fish, he yelled to his uncle. "Throw in right behind me! Hurry!"

Out of the comer of his eye, he saw George cast to the spot by the bush, then set his hook. Reeling and pumping, trying to steer the fish so as not to become entangled, they each landed a large bass within seconds of each other.

"A double," cried Jimbo excitedly, a double!"

The swollen egg-filled belly of Brad's fish indicated he had caught a spawning female, while the slightly smaller male caught by his uncle had a worn tail and was reddened from fanning the nest, proof that it was guarding its mate, perceiving the lure as a threat.

After weighing and releasing the fish, they drifted at the same depth for another hour without a strike. By this time, the sun was just peeking over the treetops, warming the air and the water, and fulfilling the promise of a cloudless, blue sky. Barely a wisp of a breeze rippled the otherwise motionless surface of the bay. Having no more luck, they stowed their gear, pulled up the trolling motor and headed for the humps they had fished before the previous day's storm. Using the same pattern proved fruitless, and as Uncle George predicted, the fishing was slow. "Slow," Brad remembered, was a term used to describe a complete lack of fishing success. He recalled that along with, "You should have been here last week," and "You're not from around here!"

They moved to a third spot. This time, they positioned the boat so that its drift would take them past main lake points, where they tried a variety of lures and techniques to no avail. They decided to try the backs of some sheltered creeks and find a place to have lunch and gas up the boat.

The creek Jimbo chose opened up from the main .lake between a sandy bluff and a low grassy knoll surrounded with submerged trees. The ones closest to the shore still had leaves on their branches. Jimbo pointed them out to Brad, indicating they were cedar trees, which he said could survive for quite some time with their "feet in the water."

"We'll fish them on our way out," Jimbo explained. "The bass like to hang around cedar trees."

Because of the direction the breeze was coming from, Jimbo said they would go all the way to the back of the creek and let the wind blow them out. Besides, there was a nice full service restaurant/gas station at the far end.

They entered the creek following a line of small orange buoys which disappeared about one-quarter of a mile in. After that, Jimbo raised the engine until only the propeller and water intake was below the surface and "putted" at slow speed, weaving through the standing trees, but alert for the sudden bump of a submerged stump. Stumps could lift the boat at an unnatural angle, causing it to slip off with a thump.

"The real danger," Jimbo commented casually, "is actually hitting a large stump with the propeller hard enough to stop the motor. It could cause internal damage to the engine."

"I can't recall being on this creek before," George said. "I don't remember any restaurant or gas dock."

"It's fairly new," Jimbo replied. "Part of the new Country Club, golf course and marina that's being built. Now that the DNR has gotten money to improve and maintain the boat lanes, some investors feel the area is about to boom. They've been buying up land and those old, rundown marinas, planning to rebuild them and add attractions for the whole family. They think times are much different than back in the early '60s when the lake was impounded. The economy's good, bass boats and fishing gear are more reliable and affordable, and fishing is more popular than ever!"

"Fishing tournaments and fishing shows on television have elevated bass fishing to the level of golf and tennis. Fishing personalities are recognized sportsmen, and there's big money involved," Brad offered.

Uncle George was staring at Jimbo with a look of awe. "Where did you hear about this supposed 'boom' on the Bend?"

"Here and there," Jimbo replied. "I hear talk. I'm not nosey. People tell me things."

They carefully picked their way toward the back of the creek. Some of the gnarled, broken trees were not more than sticks standing up from large stumps, while others were deeply pitted with holes from woodpeckers and yellow-shafted flickers, often mistaken for female redheaded woodpeckers. Still others leaned on the ones nearest to them for support. These trees were common homes for spiders, their webs forming glistening nets to trap unwary insects.

The shore, meanwhile, was a lush forest of living, healthy oaks of many varieties, cedars growing closest to the water's edge and occasionally in the river itself, due to high water from spring rains. Dogwoods and redbuds, crab apple trees and wild grapevines formed a painter s pallet of colors in their spring finery. A few leaned like the Tower of Pisa, roots clinging to the sandy soil, which was being eroded away by the rising and falling water. A careful observer could follow the old creek channel by watching the fencelike rows of trees dividing clear water from the shore. From time to time, it swung out and across, then continued on the other side.

Instead of narrowing down to a rocky niche, only carrying water after a heavy rain, the surface of the shallow water was cluttered with log jams and mats of dead vegetation. The back of the creek opened up into a vista of manicured fairways and close-clipped greens, new treated lumber boat docks with covered slips, a floating restaurant with two slips and gas pumps for fueling. The water's edge ended in a thick cedar-planked sea wall, high enough to prevent erosion at the highest lake levels, and continued down both sides to the end of the property. The bottom was dredged and cleared of potentially hazardous stumps and rocks. There were still signs of new construction, and workmen could be seen scurrying about in the throes of finishing touches and missing deadlines.

They idled slowly into one of the slips marked "Gas Only," tied off the bow and stern lines, told the casually-dressed teenager to fill the tank with the highest grade of gasoline, and asked if they could leave the boat while they had some lunch. The boy guessed it would be okay and

Jimbo, Brad and his uncle walked up the dock to the building with the words "Restaurant, Bait & Tackle" painted on the window.

Inside to the right was the bait and tackle store. Rows of perforated panels designed to hold lures and assorted tackle items, boat and motor accessories and repair parts stood in the middle of the room, not yet fully stocked. Refrigerators and freezers capable of holding ice, frozen and live bait were situated along the far wall. Several racks holding low-priced rod and reel combinations stood at the ends of the rows. By the entrance was a checkout counter. In the glass display cabinets below the counter were some electronic fish locators, marine radios and GPSs. Next to the cash register was a rack which held a variety of lake maps and a small dish filled with pennies.

To the left of the store was a room of equal size with a counter and stools along one wall, and tables and chairs filling the remainder of the floor space. The walls were hung with fish mounts advertising a local taxidermist and aerial pictures of Toledo Bend Reservoir. The hallway between the two rooms had a men's room on the left and a ladies' room on the right. Straight ahead, another door led to the covered boat slips behind the building. Jimbo, Brad and George took a table near an outside wall, so they could look out the windows which made up the top half of three walls. A few minutes later, a rather bored-looking waitress walked over carrying three glasses of water, three menus and three sets of utensils, rolled in napkins.

"The kitchen's not completely open yet," she said, sounding as if she was repeating this line for the umpteenth time. "All we got is burgers and cold sandwiches."

They all ordered cheeseburgers, French fries and cokes.

"That'll be three hamburgers, potato chips and Sprite. The Coke machine ain't hooked up yet," she corrected, her eyes fixed on something overhead only she could see.

"That will be fine," Uncle George answered politely, not wishing anything to spoil such a beautiful day. Then he got up and announced he was going to use the restroom.

"Holler if you need any help!" Brad called to him, chuckling at the absurdity of the entire scene. He pictured signs above the fixtures reading "Not hooked up yet, do not flush!," or a stall with no toilet at all, just a hole in the floor, looking down on the water.

The food came about ten minutes later, brought by the same waitress, who asked, without looking at either the tray she carried or the two men at the table, "Now, who had what?"

Brad couldn't help but think that society was doomed by the army of unskilled workers who just went through the motions of their jobs with little or no thought to customer service, satisfaction or employer loyalty. If they got fired, they simply went down the road to the next place where minimum wage personnel were hired, where they would be welcomed with open arms if they just showed up for work, occasionally were on time, did a whole day's work and didn't use the cash register as an extension of their wallet or purse.

Jimbo interrupted Brad's thoughts, saying, "Your uncle's been gone an awfully long time. His food's going to be cold. I hope he's alright. I think maybe I'll go check on him."

Brad nodded in agreement, having been deep in thought, not realizing how long George had been gone.

Sitting alone, he ate his food while watching for his uncle or Jimbo to return. From the corner of his eye, he saw Jimbo through the window, walking worriedly around the building, pausing to speak to the lad at the gas dock and looking in the boat. A few minutes later, Jimbo walked back in and sat down next to Brad.

"He's gone. I looked in the john, I looked outside, I even looked in the ladies' room. He's gone, I tell you!"

"Just take it easy," Brad said soothingly. "He couldn't have disappeared. He must have gone somewhere. Maybe he's walking along the slips looking at boats . . . Yeah, that's it, he's probably comparing boats. Let's wait here awhile. I'm sure he'll be back shortly."

Although he was not nearly as confident as he appeared for Jimbo's benefit, Brad forced himself to sit at the table and look like he was leisurely finishing his lunch, when in reality he felt as if he would throw up if he took another bite. Jimbo's eyes were everywhere, first at the clock on the wall, then the windows, the front door and the hallway to the restrooms, only to start over again. All the while, he pulled and picked at his fingers. Fifteen minutes passed and still no sign of Uncle George. Brad peeled the check from a puddle of grease accumulating on the wax paper in the bottom of the basket containing his uncle's burger. After several tries, he was able to decipher the total, which after reading, he decided the difference wasn't worth the effort of calling the waitress back to correct. Against his better judgment, he left a minimum tip, got up and walked to the register. He had intended to ask the cashier if she had seen his uncle, but thought better of it after he noticed the cashier was also their waitress.

Jimbo followed him out of the door, asking, "Now what are we going to do?"

"All we can do is ask anyone around here if they saw Uncle George. We can walk up to the clubhouse and ask around there and we can walk a ways into the woods and look around, then we can call Pat."

5

Pat stood on the dock in front of the entrance to the covered boat slips, watching the scuba diver swim from slip to slip, looking above and below to make sure a body wasn't stuck between the plastic floats that supported the walkways. She jerked her head up when she heard the yelping of the hounds straining at their leashes, as they half dragged the deputy through the woods. She had questioned the gas-dock boy, the waitress, the cook, several workmen and a fisherman whom she found sitting in his bass boat. Most of them had already talked to Brad or Jimbo, and all of them had had the same answer—they hadn't seen anything, and they didn't know anything. Later, sitting around the same table the three had come to for lunch, they discussed what they had found out, which they all knew was nothing.

"For the record, I don't believe in alien abduction," Brad said sarcastically, as Jimbo held his head in his hands, and shook it slowly from side to side.

"All I'm saying," Pat replied, "is that he's not in the woods, he's not under the water, and nobody saw him leave the dock. Those are all the facts I have to go on. You two can leave the boat here and ride back with me, or if you're taking the boat, you had better get started now, before you run out of daylight."

"The boat ride will give me a chance to think," Brad said. "Besides, it will help me get to know the lake . . . that is, if it's okay with Jimbo."

Jimbo pulled himself together enough to indicate that

he was able to drive the boat back to the factory dock.

They had to retrace their route out of the creek at barely above idle speed. By the time they got to the main lake, the sun had already dropped below the trees, their long shadows reaching far out into the boat lanes. What little breeze had blown throughout the day had died away completely, and the surface of the water was like polished ebony. Off in the distance, Brad could see the evening ritual of fish breaking the surface to grab an insect unfortunate enough to have landed on the water to rest. The snapping noise never failed to cause him to jerk around, hoping to see a huge fish break the surface. This evening, however, he found it more difficult than usual to appreciate the tranquillity of returning after a day on the water.

His thoughts kept returning to the mysterious disappearance of his uncle. How could this have happened? After all, no one could possibly have known they would be in that particular creek, in that restaurant, at that time. Hell, they didn't know themselves until they got there, and as long as it took to idle down the creek, they surely would have known if they had been followed. And as if that weren't enough, he still had no clue as to why his uncle had been targeted.

As they turned from the main lake boat lane to the mid-channel buoys leading into the bay to George's boat dock, Brad's attention again turned to the beauty of his surroundings. The old river channel ran straight up the middle of the bay, then bore off to the left, leaving a rounded peninsula with what looked like a long-overgrown old road bed directly in the center. All of the property looked like a low, rocky bluff, and formed a fairly natural sea wall without the usual dense tree growth right up to the water's edge. The water had good depth along the edge of the sea wall. The submerged timber looked like an old fence row and probably followed the old road, making access to the back of the bay easy, without the danger of random stumps or log jams. It was by far the most beautiful of the creeks or bays they had been in. What he could see of the riverfront properties were every bit as attractive as the golf course, country club and marina where his uncle disappeared. Even the site his uncle chose to build his factory on was . . . was . . . "Well, I'll be! Jimbo! Jimbo! Who owns the land around the bay besides Uncle George?"

"Well, I don't rightly know," Jimbo answered, a puzzled look on his face. "Some of it might still belong to the Army Corps of Engineers. They had to purchase all of the land before the lake was impounded, and the lake area changes as the water level fluctuates."

"But who did Uncle George buy his property from?"

"If I had to guess, I'd say the bank. Somehow or other, the bank owns everything around here, or did at one time or another. Say, what are you getting at, anyhow?"

"I don't know for sure yet," Brad answered, starting to talk as quickly as he was thinking. "But let's say, just for the sake of argument, that someone wanted all of the land around this bay for some grand project. A hotel, maybe a casino and hotel, with a marina and a few stores, or even a shopping center! And let's say that same someone was able to buy all of the land except for one large parcel with hundreds of feet of water frontage. Let's say millions of dollars were at stake and time was short. Maybe, just maybe that someone didn't want to take the time to make offers, or maybe the owner was a hard-headed old man that was happy with what he had and what he had done, and wouldn't listen to a reasonable offer!"

Jimbo picked up where Brad left off. "They might try to scare him into selling? If that didn't work, they might try to burn him out, and if that failed, he could just disappear one day and turn up dead weeks or months later, or they might dump him into an old gator hole, letting nature's vacuum cleaner with teeth take care of the loose ends."

"But there's one thing they couldn't have known," Brad continued. "Uncle George doesn't own the land, my father does . . . or did, anyway. Now, I own it! If our guess is right, doing away with Uncle George won't get them what they want. But we have to find him before they kill him for nothing!"

"Some choice," Jimbo said solemnly. "Find your uncle before they kill him, so they can try to kill you instead. Maybe I'd better come home with you tonight, just in case someone tries to contact you about your uncle, or decides that no Allens are better than one."

Not taking no for an answer, Jimbo followed closely behind Brad for the rest of the drive to George's house. Brad had decided to call Pat immediately and share his suppositions with her. It was pitch dark by the time they reached the house. With only a small motion-sensing light on the outside of the house, Brad and Jimbo felt their way tentatively into the front door. Brad thought it fortunate that his uncle always left his house keys in his pickup truck while they were fishing, not taking a chance on dropping them in the water. Fumbling for the light switch, Brad nearly tripped over the sprawling pile of mail beneath the front door mail slot.

"Make yourself at home," Brad said. "Look in the fridge if you need a beer, and help yourself to the TV. I'll just toss this pile of mail on the table, then I'll call Pat."

As he reached for the letters, he subconsciously sorted

them according to size. The last one on the floor was a plain legal-sized envelope. He picked it up, noticing that it was unsealed. Thinking it was third class advertising, he was about to toss it on the pile with the rest when he noticed it carried no stamp. Taking a closer look, he saw only the words BRAD ALLEN written on the envelope. Looking back at the door, he reasoned that this letter was dropped into the slot prior to the regular mail delivery. He made a mental note to find out what time the mail was usually delivered. Suddenly realizing that there could be fingerprints on the envelope and its contents, he dropped it on the floor as close as he could to where he found it. Brad walked through the family room, passing Jumbo, who was trying to work the remote control to turn on the television. On the other side of the room, Brad picked up the phone and dialed the sheriff s office.

The voice on the other end announced he had reached the Hemphill Sheriff's Department, and asked how she could direct his call. "This is Brad Allen calling. May I please speak with the sheriff? . . . No, I would not care to leave a message, but could you have her return my call as soon as she gets in? . . . Yes, it is an emergency! She has my number."

Hanging up the phone, he told Jimbo about the envelope he had found on the floor.

"I have a gut feeling that that envelope contains some information about my uncle. I believe he's still alive. I just hope he stays that way until the sheriff gets back to us, so we can look inside without damaging the evidence."

Jimbo stopped channel surfing and wondered aloud if the envelope contained a ransom note made from words cut out of old newspapers and magazines.

Brad was about to comment on Jimbo's idea when he heard the approaching wail of a police siren. He got to his feet in time to watch a squad car pull into the driveway. The siren stopped, and Pat jumped out of the car. She headed for the front door on the run, her right hand resting on the handle of her revolver.

"What's going on?" she demanded, her eyes looking past Brad and taking in all she could see in the lighted rooms. "They told me it was an emergency, so I didn't waste time returning your call."

Pat stepped into the room. Pointing to the envelope on the floor, Brad told her that he had handled the envelope before he realized it wasn't part of the regular mail, and that he had then replaced it on the floor. After noting the envelope's position in her notebook, she went back out to the squad car and opened the trunk. Pat removed a yellow plastic case, reentered the house and set the case on a convenient table.

"This is my 'ick' kit," she explained, as she opened the case and removed a pair of surgical gloves. "Among other things, I use these gloves so I don't contaminate the evidence with my fingerprints."

Pat carried the letter into the family room followed closely by Brad, who joined Jimbo at the large table. She carefully removed the contents, which consisted of a folded legal-sized sheet of paper. It read, "We have your uncle, George Allen. If you want to see him alive, it will cost you one hundred and fifty thousand dollars. You will be contacted later with further instructions. Contact the police or ignore any of these instructions, and you will never see him again."

Pat held the letter up to the light and examined it closely.

"The problem is," she explained, "this was typed on a computer, and printed with a standard inkjet printer. Not a chance in the world of tracing it back to where it was written. I'll certainly check it out, but I would be willing to bet we won't find any fingerprints except yours. Now, I know what you're going to say, but believe me, we have nothing to go on. We have to wait until whoever it is contacts you, and hope they make a mistake. You'd better go through the motions, because so far they seem to have all of their bases covered. I hope this house isn't being watched, the way I came screaming up here. We'll have to be more discreet in the future.

With that, she gathered up the letter and its envelope, said she'd be in touch, and walked out the door. This time she made no big show of leaving, and drove swiftly but quietly away.

Jimbo sat and stared as Brad closed the door and walked back to the table. He didn't sit, but paced up and down the length of the family room.

"That all you're goin' to do?" Jimbo asked.

"What do you mean?" Brad replied.

"Last year, I had occasion to call the sheriff on account of this bar across the road from my house. Now I'm not against bars. I've stopped in them myself now and again. But this here one gets real noisy about three in the morning pretty regular. The music is real loud, too, and there's a lot of fights outside. I wouldn't mind it early in the evening, but at three in the morning, it breaks up my sleep. Well, a couple of times, I called the sheriff and she sent her deputies over to quiet things down. I don't blame her for that, 'cause it's sure no place for a woman, even a policewoman. When the deputies left, they started whooping it up all over again. So I called over there and told the bartender to quite things down a bit so I could get my sleep. What he had to say wasn't very polite. I called him again and told him who I was, because I didn't think he realized the first time I called or he wouldn't have been so nasty. You know, that old boy used some words I ain't never heard before."

Brad saw an odd gleam in Jimbo's eye as he warmed to his theme.

"Well now, I figured the only way I was going to get some rest was to go over there myself and make sure they understood me real clear. I got this aluminum club, like a small baseball bat. It's used for hitting fish on the head to kill them, so they don't squirm around and dirty up a boat. I don't take it with me fishing anymore, what with catch and release. Anyhow, I took my bat and walked across the street. First thing I did was to fetch that bartender over the bar to get his attention. Then three or four hardcases objected to my turning off the jukebox. I know if they hadn't been drinking, they never would have been that unreasonable. I convinced them to come around to my way of thinking. I even offered to drive them to the hospital for stitches. You know, ever since then, it's been real quiet after midnight and that bartender, he's very respectful. Whenever I see him, he smiles at me. He even looks better now with his new teeth! Yessir, sometimes you just have to take matters into your own hands to get them done right."

Jimbo told the story with such sincerity, that Brad was sure it happened exactly the way he related it.

"But what's that got to do with Uncle George's kidnapping?"

"Look," Jimbo reasoned, "whoever's responsible for snatching your uncle couldn't have been working alone. And if we assume that the same people are responsible for everything that's been happening to this point, at least some of them have to be locals. They'd have to be to get around as good as they've been. I'd rule out people like the minister and the school teachers, if you get my drift.

So, my idea is this: we visit a few of the local establishments, talk to some of the boys, reason with them, and see if we can't find someone who is willing to talk nice to us." When Brad readily agreed, Jimbo suggested that they leave immediately. "The joints ought to be jumpin' by now."

Climbing into Jimbo's truck, Brad asked him where he thought the kidnappers might be keeping his uncle.

"You know, I've been giving that a lot of thought ever since I saw that letter. Partly, it depends on whether they keep him alive or not. I could tell better if I knew who was involved. Some of the no-account locals tend to stay to a certain area."

Brad told Jimbo that he would go to the bank as soon as it opened the next morning, see how much money his uncle had in his account, and like Pat suggested, go through the motions.

The first place they turned into on their mission appeared to have been converted from something else into a tavern. Brad said as much to Jimbo, who replied that many businesses went broke and the buildings were rented out as bars or liquor stores.

"Seems like the only kind of business that never goes broke."

Cars and pickup trucks were parked all along the front of the building, so they had to pull around the side and park on a well-used strip of grass. They could hear the sound of the jukebox playing a country tune. The front door was standing open and Brad could see a haze of cigarette smoke hanging in the air The two men walked into the manmade fog.

To the right was a pool table, and to the left was a bar that followed the wall all the way to the end and curved to return about half way back. At its end was a postage stamp-sized dance floor, where two couples were trying to line dance to the tune playing. Men and women standing and sitting at the bar turned to follow Brad and Jimbo with their eyes. The couples on the dance floor stopped and stood watching. The pool players backed away from the table and stood up straight, looking at the two.

"Is it me?" Brad asked. "Do I stand out that much? I find it hard to believe that everyone in every bar we enter knows instinctively that I'm not from around here."

"Did I mention that I live across the street?" Jimbo asked flippantly. "I'm going to talk to the boys playing pool. Get yourself a drink at the bar, but keep your eyes and ears open."

Brad found and claimed an empty stool. With one foot on the rail and the other on the floor, he turned sideways so he could watch Jimbo as he approached the pool table. The bartender, a heavy-set fellow with perennial beads of perspiration along his receding hairline and armpit stains on his white shirt, waddled on down. He gave Brad the once over, then glared at Jimbo. His rolled up sleeves revealed tattoos advertising a branch of the military service on one forearm and a reference to someone's "Mother" on the other. He didn't smile, so Brad wondered if he was the same one Jimbo had had words with.

"I don't want any trouble from you guys so why don't you get Jimbo and get out of here!"

Trying not to be antagonistic, Brad replied, "Look we just came in for a drink and a little information."

"Well, you're not going to get either," the big man said, grabbing Brad by the front of his shirt.

The bartender had a vicelike grip, which Brad thought probably came in handy for twisting the tops off beer bottles, but he was slow. With one quick motion, Brad put his hand over the one holding him by the shirt, grasped the thumb, and bent it back. The excruciating pain brought tears to the bartender's eyes.

"You could buy a new set of teeth, but you won't be able to steal money from the register without this thumb," Brad growled. He guided the limp hand from his shirt, the thumb bent back at a sickening angle. Brad glanced over to see Jimbo pinning a man against the pool table, holding the cue like a sword. He released the bartender's thumb, and the big man wobbled to the ice maker, holding his thumb as if he were afraid it would fall off. Brad stepped from the bar to join Jimbo walking out of the door.

"Nothing," Jimbo replied to Brad's unasked question. "Frankly, this is too high-class a place. I would've been really surprised if we found out anything here."

They climbed back into Jimbo's truck, made a U-turn in the grass, and pulled out onto the road. "By the way," Jimbo continued, "you handled yourself pretty well back there. They won't forget what you did tonight. Those kind of people respect that."

Two more bars and one roadhouse later, they were no closer to finding Uncle George than they had been before. Brad ordered drinks while Jimbo found the people most likely to have some information. The only encouraging thing was that they didn't have to fight their way out of any of the establishments.

Sitting in the parking lot of the Dew Drop Inn, Jimbo said, "Something keeps eating at me. The way Tucker Jones and his boys started that ruckus out at Dolly's place. He couldn't have known your uncle from the man in the moon, and unless someone told him, he wouldn't have known he owned Caliente. The more I think on it, I believe they were at Dolly's working out the plan to kidnap George. I think it was a coincidence that we stumbled in there when we did, and when he figured out who we were, decided to revise his plan. He probably thought with his gang outnumbering us, it would be easy to beat you and me senseless, and take your uncle in all the commotion. He didn't figure on you bein' so handy in a fight. I know Tucker. He's a bully and a coward, but certainly not smart enough to organize a job like this on his own. Get him by himself, and he'll tell us who the brains are behind him."

Brad had to admit that Jimbo's scenario made sense, so they found a phone booth and, late as it was, he dialed Pat's home number. After several rings, she picked up the receiver and in between yawns told Brad that a local lawyer paid Tucker's fine and damages, so she had to release him. "Now, what's so all-fired important that it couldn't wait 'til morning?"

"Sorry to have disturbed you," Brad answered. "Go back to sleep, and I'll meet you at the diner for breakfast to tell you all about it." Before she had a chance to reply, he hung the phone up and returned to the truck to tell Jimbo the news.

6

George Allen awoke with a great ringing in his ears. The pain he felt came from an area at the back of his head. He had the giddy thought that he'd been hit on the head so many times that his head was really a large baseball. Reaching back to feel for the seams, his hand came back with sticky red blood on it.

As the pain increased, his memory started to flood back. He remembered going to the men's room, seeing the "OUT OF ORDER" sign, and walking out the back doors toward the boat slips to look for an outdoor restroom. The next thing he knew, he was here, wherever here was.

Moving slowly into a sitting position, he realized he wasn't restrained. What he could see of the room looked to be rectangular in shape, about nine feet wide and twelve feet long. When he tried to get to his feet, a wave of nausea passed over him and he felt dizzy. His giddiness returned, and chuckling to himself, he thought he probably had a slight concussion.

The windows were covered with curtains that looked like some sort of canvas material, tacked over the window openings with roofing nails. From what little light filtered through the tears in the material and the loose or cracked boards in the walls, he guessed it must be close to sundown.

His eyes had become accustomed to the dim light, and as the pain and dizziness subsided, he took stock of his situation. The room was little more than a shack and probably not weatherproofed. The cobwebs that hung like tinsel from the exposed timbers and the mountains of dead insects on the rickety old kitchen table at one side of the room suggested a long period of neglect, and he did not dismiss the possibility of total abandonment.

He moved cautiously about the room, stopping with each wave of unsteadiness until it waned. Suddenly, he realized it wasn't only him that was unsteady, but the room itself was rocking gently as he moved. Feeling his way along the perimeter of the room, he found the door. Next to it, he felt a rusted electrical box containing what he hoped was a light switch. He flipped it up and down, but nothing happened. Exploring the outer edges of the door, he came upon the doorknob. Turning it slowly at first, then forcefully, he concluded it was locked from the outside.

He had made enough noise rattling the door that he decided he was quite alone, so putting his shoulder down, he used all of his considerable bulk to try to open the door. This time, the door flew open with a splintering of wood, and he spilled out onto what looked like a small deck running completely around the shack. As the sun dipped below the horizon, he realized that he was on a homemade pontoon boat, probably used at one time to tow over a good crappie hole. By tying off to some stickups, its inhabitants could fish with all of the comforts of home. At one time, it might have been suitable to live aboard for several days. But now, it was one of many such crappie shacks. Abandoned in a weed-choked stump field away from the boat lanes, and left to decay and sink, it would ultimately provide more structure for fish.

Looking about him in the fading daylight, he could see that he was in the middle of a huge submerged forest of silvery skeletons. Each one cast strange, changing shadows on the peeling white paint of his watery prison, and on the liquid surface, polished to a mirrorlike finish with the dying evening breeze. Far off in the distance, what he perceived as land could easily have been a shallow island of rushes. He might as well have been on the moon.

He went back inside to avoid the hungry evening insects that swarmed about his exposed skin. Now fully alert, his thoughts turned to food and drink. Finding none, he decided that keeping him alive and well was not high on someone's list of priorities. He thought back to when he was a teenager, when he had dreamed of adventure and heroism. In his twenties and thirties, he had dreamed of adventure and heroism. In his forties and fifties, he had dreamed of adventure, but the heroism had been tempered with the knowledge of his own weaknesses. Now, he just wanted to survive. He could drink the water from the lake, but food was another matter. He hoped the weather would stay mild, but for the present he decided to find a comfortable place on the floor and try to sleep, thinking things might look better in the morning.

It was late by the time Brad and Jimbo got to Dolly's place. Stepping out of the truck, Brad couldn't help but notice the moon was nearly full. If they ever got to fish the tournament, it would be within a day before or after a full moon, which was supposedly the best fishing time. He was surprised he could think of such things at a time like this.

"One of us should go around to guard the back door, in case he tries to run, provided of course he's in there," observed Jimbo.

"I'll go," Brad said. He walked toward the rear of the building. Moving carefully in the moonlight, Brad rounded the back side, trying to make his eyes adjust to the low light. Suddenly, the back door opened and a figure stepped out into the gloom. Throwing caution to the wind, Brad charged. With his head tucked to the side, he made contact with his muscular shoulder, wrapping his arm around the body as he drove forward and down. He lay on top of the body with his arm underneath, hesitating long enough for his breathing to get back to normal. During those few seconds, he realized that the soft body parts he was holding could not possibly belong to Tucker Jones. Getting quickly to his knees and rolling the limp form over, he looked into the unconscious face of Dolly. He put his hand to her throat and felt a strong pulse in her neck. His next thought was to make sure she could breathe well enough, but as far down as her shirt was unbuttoned, he didn't think that would be a problem. He was on the verge of panic when she started to moan and move her head from side to side, her eyes fluttering.

"Wha—what happened?" she moaned.

Jimbo waited at the front of Dolly's place, giving Brad enough time to work his way around and find a good position in the back. After a fair time, Jimbo opened the door and stepped cautiously into the dim, dingy interior. He tried to put himself in Tucker's place: would he lay low and make himself scarce until the plot was carried out, or would he go on with his miserable existence as if nothing had happened?

He didn't have a chance to answer himself, because as he scanned the booths and tables, he saw a tall, thin man hurriedly get up and run for the kitchen door. He was closely followed by two other men, who stopped at the door, turned, and set themselves to stop anyone attempting to follow In three long, quick strides, Jimbo was across the room, facing two very determined-looking thugs.

Brad put his arm behind Dolly's shoulders, and began to gently lift her while he apologized desperately. Suddenly, the rear door flew open, and Tucker Jones came out at a full run. Not expecting anything or anyone to be in the way, he smashed into the kneeling body of Brad and the recovering body of Dolly. The three tumbled into a pile of tangled arms and legs. Brad was up at once. After several years of playing football, he was used to unraveling himself from piles of bodies. A quick glance at Dolly told him that she was out cold again. Tucker Jones madly tried to regain his footing, but Brad was on him like a cat. With a lightning move, he bent Tucker's left arm behind his back, hooking it through his own right arm so that any attempt to struggle would cause painful strain and possibly even serious injury, if he was determined.

The door flew open once more. This time, Jimbo looked tentatively through the opening.

"See to Dolly," Brad ordered, pointing to the prone body stretched out next to a magnolia tree. "By the way, what took you so long?"

"There are a couple of boys inside that didn't take likely to me following Tucker through the kitchen," Jimbo replied, breathing heavily. "They're going to be on a liquid diet for a few weeks after they wake up. Take Tucker out to the truck and wait for me while I carry Dolly in and make sure she's okay."

Jimbo lifted Dolly and carried her as if she were a rag doll into the kitchen. He laid her gently on a length of counter, and rummaged through the cupboards underneath the sink for some ammonia. Finding a half empty bottle, he took a dish rag and poured a small amount of the contents on it. He made a wad of the cloth, and wafted it under her nose. Dolly immediately began to cough and move. She looked around, sat up slowly, and held her head in her hands. Everything had happened so fast, she still had no idea what had taken place, and she began to whimper softly.

"I just went outside to get a breath of fresh air," she moaned. "What happened?"

Jimbo didn't have the time or inclination to tell her the long version, so he lied. "I found you lying on the ground out in back. You must have fainted."

"I need a drink."

Jimbo nodded, then walked into the bar. He kept walking, stepping over the unconscious bodies which no one in the place had paid any attention to, until he got to his pickup truck. There Brad sat, still holding Tucker's arm. Jimbo climbed in, pushing hard against Tucker, as he started the engine and reached for the gearshift.

"What's going on here? Where are you taking me? You won't get away with this! I ain't done nothing! You're breaking my arm!" Tucker whined as they started down the road.

Jimbo was right. Tucker Jones was a bully and a coward. As they drove along, he kept repeating his metaphors, his voice getting higher and shriller, panic beginning to set in. Brad and Jimbo were no help to him, as they sat silent, only acknowledging his presence with an occasional surly look. In fact, Brad had no idea where they were going or what they were going to do with Tucker. Jimbo drove for nearly half an hour before turning off the two-lane blacktop onto a deeply rutted trail of sand and clay that twisted and turned. When it looked as if the path ended in the beam of the headlights, it actually split into two sharp curves to the left and right. The trees, mostly firs, grew right to the edge of the trail, and from time to time Brad could see where the roots of one were cut through by the machine that cored out the road. He also thought it was probably a good thing that the base was sandy, judging by the amount of water in the ruts and low spots. During a wet spell, the way would be impassable in all but four-wheel-drive vehicles. Finally, Jimbo brought the truck to a stop at a point where the trail went no further, but widened enough for a vehicle to turn around. The truck's bright lights revealed a short footpath through the woods, leading back to the water's edge.

"Well, this is the end of the road," Jimbo exclaimed.

"Where are we?" Brad asked, as he watched Tucker's eyes widen with fright.

"This is the back of a creek called Coal Miner's Cove," Jimbo replied. "Local fishing guides bring their customers back in here by boat if they want to see alligators. The sand and clay in the soil banks get undercut by the action of the water, and the gators just naturally use them for dens. When the weather's warm, you'll see them all out around this creek during the day. They look like old truck tires, just barely floating above the surface. But don't be fooled, they can move mighty quick if they're of a mind to. Occasionally, they'll even come through the woods or over the roads, if there's something good for them to eat . . . and they'll eat just about anything."

Brad could hear Tucker's quick intake of breath, followed by a gulp. Jimbo stepped out of the truck, then reached back in and grabbed Tucker by the front of his shirt. With no regard to his protests as he hit the steering wheel, Jimbo half-lifted, half-dragged him out of the cab, and slammed him against the side of the bed.

"Now then, it's time we had a nice little talk. First, you'll tell us where George Allen is, then who's pulling your strings, and if we like your answers, maybe we won't leave you here, tied to a tree for gator bait," Jimbo hissed, sounding positively diabolical.

Summoning his last ounce of courage, Tucker Jones replied, "I ain't got nothin' to say!"

"So be it," Jimbo crowed. Acting as if he were really enjoying himself, he busied himself extracting a rope from behind the front seat of the truck. He then proceeded to tie Tucker securely to a tree within sight of the trail and the water's edge. Testing the knots, he explained that they would check back come morning, and if he was still alive, maybe he'd feel more like talking.

As they turned the truck around and started to drive away, Brad could hear inhuman shrieking, which faded to an incoherent blubbering as all sounds were lost in the noise of the engine, and of the tires bounding in the ruts.

"I hope you know what you're doing," Brad said tentatively.

Jimbo assured him that this early in the year, evening temperatures dipped low enough to keep any self-respecting alligator snug in his den. "Hopefully," Jumbo added, "Tucker don't know that."

The morning broke clear and bright. The weatherman predicted several days of stable weather, due to a stalled high pressure area over the entire southwest. But the possibility for a sudden change could occur with the passage of a frontal system. Brad interpreted this to mean that the sun would shine today, but tomorrow was anybody's guess. The only thing he knew for sure was that forty-eight hours of consistently good weather meant good fishing.

He got into Jimbo's truck, backed out of the driveway, and headed for town. He hoped to catch Pat at the diner, where he could explain what he and Jimbo were trying to do, find out if she had any more news about his uncle's kidnapping, and discuss his plan for getting the ransom money. Jimbo and he had already decided that Brad would come into town, while Jimbo went back out to Coal Miner's Cove in George's truck to collect Tucker Jones. They further agreed to bring Tucker back to town and let the sheriff try her luck, if he still refused to talk.

The morning sun beat mercilessly on the tin roof of the abandoned crappie shack, making it oppressively hot inside. George awoke with sweat puddling around his nose and running down his neck. He opened his eyes to get his first good look at his prison. He hoped at first it was all a dream, but the perspiration stinging his eyes was real enough, as was the growing thirst beginning to gnaw at him. He staggered to his feet, feeling every sore spot on his body. He opened the door and limped out onto the small deck, feeling the air remove some of the moisture from his clothing and skin.

He tried to remember how he came to be in this place and who was responsible, but the thoughts refused to come. In all likelihood, he never saw the person or persons who brought him here. The one thing he knew for sure was that he was thirsty. Thirsty enough to drink the lake water. Lying flat on the narrow deck, he leaned his head over far enough to reach the water. Looking down into the stained water, he began to chuckle. The chuckle became a laugh and soon he had to roll over and clutch his stomach to keep himself from the pain the laughter was causing. Rising up to within about two feet of the surface was hydrilla. So thick in spots, he could see nests with huge spawning female bass in the middle of them right on the top of the grass. Around and under the old pontoons, he saw dozens of large bass suspended, probably males waiting for a female to leave so they could swim in and guard her eggs or drive away intruders. The irony of his situation, plus the fact that there were more than enough big bass around this one shack to win the tournament, was more than he could handle.

7

Brad entered the diner and looked for Pat. Being the only sit-down restaurant in town that served breakfast, he was sure he was in the right place. The booths held the typical breakfast crowd in a town near a sport fishing lake. The casual fishermen who can't seem to wake up before sunrise and expects the fish to exhibit the same human characteristics; the family fisherman who doesn't want his family to get out on the water without a good healthy breakfast; the "You should have been here yesterday" fishermen, who sit around the table, ordering coffee and talking loudly for hours about yesterday's experiences; and finally, small groups of truck drivers who adopt a particular diner for their morning coffee break stop.

There was no sign of Pat. Perhaps he had just gotten there too early. He took a stool at the counter, where he could keep his eye on the front door, and looked at a menu. He mentally expressed his disappointment at not finding a hand written or typewritten page ensconced in a clear plastic cover describing their culinary offerings. Even small town diners had gone high-tech: the menu, changed daily, was computer printed. Healthy heart be damned, he thought, a good fisherman eats the "Fisherman's Special": two eggs any style (fried in bacon grease), two pancakes, two strips of bacon, two sausages, juice and coffee. The service was fast and friendly, the food was good and the price was reasonable. Sharing it with Pat would have made his enjoyable morning even better.

But it was not to be. A strange feeling of anguish crept over him as he got up to pay the bill. He shook it off as he walked out into the warm sunshine and headed down the street to the bank.

Walking up to the door of the bank, Brad noticed a poster in the sidelight to the right of the door. It read "Hemphill Bank And Trust is a proud sponsor of the Annual Caliente Boat Company Fishing Tournament." It included the times, dates and rules of the contest. He was amazed that he hadn't noticed it the last time he was here. As he stood reading, his eye caught movement over the top of the board.

He saw a familiar figure walking out of the office of Reed Hadley. Hadley had his left arm hooked loosely through her right and it bumped against the grip of her pistol as they walked. They turned and faced each other. Pat shook Hadley's hand, then headed toward the door. Brad slipped around one of the large supporting columns as she walked out of the door. He wasn't sure why he declined to face her, but he knew his uncle wasn't the only Allen who disliked Reed Hadley.

At first, his thoughts raced over why Pat had come to see him. But he quickly realized he was acting like a jealous fool. There were a thousand reasons for a sheriff to see the bank president. Maybe she was telling him about his uncle's kidnapping and showing him the ransom note.

Brad entered the bank and approached the information desk, but before he could request an audience with Reed Hadley, the man took his hand. Steering Brad into his office, the bank president offered him a chair. Taking his own overstuffed leather wing chair, Hadley rested his elbows on the desktop and made his fingers into a tent.

In his well-oiled voice, Hadley asked, "What can I do for you, Mr. Allen?"

"I'd like to get the total of my uncle's liquid assets, and would you possibly know if he has any money or negotiable stocks or bonds in any other banks?" Brad asked this in his most businesslike manner.

"It will take some time to print out that information. You do, of course, have some type of document giving you power of attorney?"

"Well, no. Not exactly. That is, I—" Brad stammered.

"I'm sorry, then," Hadley rejoined, gazing stonily at Brad. "I'm not at liberty to give you any information regarding your uncle's financial affairs."

Brad tried again. "Look, my uncle has been kidnapped. For all we know, he may be dead. We've received a ransom note asking for one hundred and fifty thousand dollars. I need to know if he has that kind of money. The sheriff will verify my story, and she has the ransom note."

Hadley persisted, "Mr. Allen, this is a small town, the kind that's used to doing business on a handshake. But in a case like this, my hands are tied. Without your uncle sitting there next to you, so we could be absolutely sure of his intentions, legally I can do nothing. And if you can prove he's deceased, his will would have to go through probate, and then his lawful heirs will have access to the information you're seeking. Until such time, as cold and heartless as it sounds, I truly am sorry," he said as he stood, indicating that the interview was over.

Brad raised himself to his full height and said in a voice he did not recognize, "Listen, I'm not interested in this legal bullshit! This is my uncle's life we're talking about, and I know damn well you can figure some way around it!"

Hadley composed himself, and in his smoothest tone said, "Please, Mr. Allen, please sit. I hesitated to bring up one possibility, because I'm not sure it won't betray a confidence."

"Go on."

"The other day, when you and your uncle were here, he mentioned you were the lawful owner of the property his factory was built on. That being the case, I could see my way clear to make a loan. That is the bank would make a loan in the amount of one hundred and fifty thousand dollars, using the deed to the property as collateral. After your uncle is released, say within ten days, he should be able to pay the money back, plus a nominal fee for the use of the money for ten days, of course."

"Of course," Brad echoed. "And if my uncle is killed, or not released within ten days, the property is forfeited."

"Of course," Hadley repeated. "But that's our only option. Take it or leave it."

Now the meeting was really over. As Brad walked out of his office, Hadley held out his hand with a beneficent look on his face. It was no wonder, Brad thought as he brushed past the outstretched hand, that people around here lived in near poverty. With bankers like Hadley, an honest person wouldn't have a chance.

"I'll let you know," Brad said over his shoulder, and walked out of the bank.

Brad decided to stop at the sheriff's office on his way back to his uncle's house, to tell Pat how he made out at the bank, and to see if Jimbo had brought Tucker Jones in. When he pulled into the parking lot, he saw his uncle's truck, with a crowd of people standing around it. Deputies made up most of the crowd. He parked as close as he could and walked toward the truck, sighting Jimbo and Pat in the crowd as he got closer.

From the size of the crowd, Brad thought Jimbo must have brought Tucker Jones back. An astonished look appeared on his face as he saw Tucker's body in the bed of the pickup truck, a red stain on the front of his bib overalls. Blood was dripping slowly from the corner of the tailgate. The wail of a siren broke his concentration as an ambulance raced toward the crowd, scattering deputies and gawkers as it backed to the truck.

Two uniformed men jumped out of the rear doors, unfolding a gurney as they lowered the tailgate of the pickup. One of them produced a sheet and covered the body. With practiced efficiency, they moved the body to the ambulance and after a brief conversation with Pat, drove off. The excitement ended, the crowd slowly dispersed until only Pat and Jimbo, with Brad still in a state of shock, stood in the parking lot. Brad heard the phrases "thorough investigation" and "released on your own recognizance," then "Don't attempt to leave town" before he could get his feet to move toward them.

He said haltingly, "What happened?"

"What's it look like happened?" Pat snapped. "Jimbo killed Tucker!"

Jimbo replied sullenly, "It was self-defense."

"Did he talk? Did he say anything about Uncle George?" Brad asked, his voice rising.

"No!"

"'No? That's all you can say? For God's sake, my uncle could be buried alive or locked in a closet somewhere, and you kill the only one likely to have the key and all I hear is 'no'!"

Pat interrupted Brad. "Take it easy! Flying off at Jimbo isn't going to bring Tucker back. Besides, if it happened the way Jimbo claims, it was clearly self-defense. Rest assured, I'm going to investigate this thoroughly."

Brad barely heard her finish as he spun around and ran back to the old truck, jumped in and sped away. He drove on, not really paying attention to where he was going. His mind was a whirlwind of thoughts and emotions. He had no one to turn to, no one to help him. He had trusted and believed everybody, now he could trust and believe nobody. His uncle had trusted Jimbo with his life. But Jimbo had talked him into going to town this morning, while he went to get Tucker. Could he possibly have wanted to silence Tucker?

Perhaps it was Jimbo all along who was behind the scheme. Jimbo knew when his uncle was flying out, and where the truck would be left. He could even have had a key to get in. He was the first one at the factory after it burned. He could easily have set an explosive device after business hours, and sat in the garage to watch it burn. He was known and trusted by the locals. Did he conspire with Tucker Jones to kidnap George Allen and hold him for ransom? No one would pay attention to him rummaging about his uncle's house while he cut the gas pipe. What did his uncle really know about his background? Jimbo had just appeared one day and asked for a job. It wouldn't be the first time a good deed was repaid by an evil one.

And how about the sheriff? She didn't appear to be working too hard to solve the case. For that matter, it could be someone Brad hadn't met yet. Perhaps the owner of the marina and country club where his uncle disappeared wanted him out of the way, so they could get his property. Brad pulled over to the side of the road and brought the truck to a stop. He leaned forward and banged his head against the steering wheel out of frustration. What was he going to do now? He wasn't a detective. He was little more than a kid. Never before had Brad felt more afraid and alone.

Brad didn't know how long he sat with his head

against the steering wheel before his head cleared, but having temporarily vented his frustrations, he decided he needed to focus on helping his uncle no matter what obstacles were put in his path. Making a U-turn across the road, he tried to retrace his route back to where he recognized some landmarks. Once he got into town, he knew he could find his way back to his uncle's house. Along the way, he passed the all-too-familiar sheriffs office, bank, and, just before the square, the courthouse.

He moved his lips. "The courthouse, of course!"

He parked the truck in one of the angled spaces outside the rusted wrought iron fence surrounding the old courthouse. Climbing the well-worn granite steps, he noticed the date on the cornerstone, indicating that it had been built in 1896. He gazed upwards, taking in the heavily Southwest-influenced architecture of the structure, noting how out-of-place the air-conditioners looked jutting from the tall, thin windows. He wondered how the city fathers weighed the expense of updating this relic with electricity and running water, and later computer network wiring, handicapped access and elevators, compared with tearing it down and rebuilding a modern functional office building. He supposed a lot of emotion and local politics were involved.

He walked through the massive doors, which led into an atrium. A once-intricate painting, now faded and peeling, spread across the high vaulted ceiling. Brad was struck by the purpose of it all. It was meant to intimidate the person entering, and subjugate him to the authority of the building and what went on within. It might have accomplished just that in its first thirty or forty years, but today, Brad wondered what effect it had, when they could barely get the doors to sit in the badly sagging and out-of-square jambs.

On his right, a small sign stood out from the wall, indicating that the County Clerk, County Assessor and Office of Deeds and Records was inside the room next to it. He entered this room, and approached the high wooden counter that separated the public from the desks arranged in pods behind it. The front of the counter, with its once-ornate raised panels and millwork, was painted gloss white to hide the wear and tear and for ease of maintenance. The desks and office equipment were modern, complete with a desktop computer at each station. A printer clicked and hummed away busily in the background. Brad's trained eye followed the myriad of water pipes, bundles of computer cables and lines of surface mold, bringing power and carrying signals back and forth, up and down, from ceiling lights to telephone wires duct taped to the floor between desks for safety. Checking out the wiring with professional interest, he failed to notice the older, pleasant-looking woman approach the counter until she asked in a soft Southern drawl, "Can I help y'all?"

With something of a start, he began. "I'm not from around here, but I own some property on the lake. I wonder if it would be possible to look at a plat of survey of the bay, to see who owns the adjoining land."

She told him it would be much easier if he had the legal description of his parcel's location, but if he could recognize the area from a lake map, she could most likely narrow it down. She first showed him a topographical map of the entire lake and surrounding area, indicating compass directions and their present location. He had no trouble finding the bay on which his uncle's factory once stood. Pointing it out to her, she carefully noted the section number then refolded the map.

She then went over to a deep, ancient-looking wall

shelving unit with wood-framed glass doors. Opening the doors revealed several large and dusty books. She found the one she was looking for, carried it with obvious effort to the counter, and set it down.

The yellowed pages she leafed through were actually old engineering surveys, bound together to form the books. So much, Brad thought, for high-tech. She stopped at the page corresponding to the section number she had noted and turned the book so Brad could view the page.

"You must understand that some of the parcels have no name, just a number," she explained. "Also, some of the names would have changed, due to sales transactions. The corrections don't necessarily appear until the deed is brought up-to-date. It's not a requirement if the land has passed through an estate. However, we keep those records on the computer and if the property changed hands in the last ten years, I can easily look up the current owner."

Brad saw the name "Allen" neatly lettered in the middle of the piece of the plat he recognized as his uncle's factory site. Unfortunately, each of the other lots had only a number designation.

"Would it be a lot of trouble to try to find out who owns the other lots on the cove?" he asked.

The lady said she would check the computer. She put a scrap of paper in the page to mark it, and heaved the book to her chest. She walked to a vacant desk, set it down with a thump, and reopened it. She took a seat in front of the computer and began a staccato tattoo on the keyboard. She stopped every so often to jot some words down on a note pad.

In a short while, she came back to the counter and said, "That was easy. The same corporation owns all of the land except yours and the piece directly adjoining yours to the west. Here are the names. I wrote them down for you."

Brad thanked the lady for her time and effort. He folded the slip of paper, put it in his pocket, turned and walked out of the office and the building.

When he got back to the truck, he retrieved the paper and read the names: Frank du Boise and Haley Deer Corporation. Neither name meant anything to Brad. If only Uncle George were here, Brad thought. These names might mean something to him. He started the truck and drove back to the house.

Pulling into the driveway next to his uncle's truck, Brad saw that it was dripping wet. The bed showed no sign of blood. He walked to the front door and tried the handle. The door opened and he cautiously entered. He followed the sound of the television to find Jimbo sitting in his uncle's recliner, watching The Weather Channel.

"You've got some nerve coming back here! And how the hell did you get in, anyway?"

"You left the house keys on the front seat of the truck. Look Brad, I had to explain how it happened. You took off in such a hurry, I didn't get a chance. I can imagine what you must be thinking." He paused in his narrative, the air thick with tension.

"Go on," Brad sulked.

"When I got to where we left Tucker, he was nowhere to be seen. From where I was sitting, I could see the coils of rope still around the tree he was tied to. At first, I thought maybe a gator got him. But there was no blood and no sign of a struggle. What's more, the ropes looked like they were cut. I didn't think somebody just stumbled across him and helped him to escape. He must have had a knife hidden in his boot and used it to cut the ropes and free himself. Even so, it would have been too far to try and walk out, especially at night.

"That's when I started to worry. He knew we would come back this morning to try and get him to talk. He was a bully and a coward, but he was also poison mean, and I just felt him waiting, hiding out there to try and kill me when I got out of the truck. I looked around inside the cab for something I could use for a weapon. Then, I found the small pistol your uncle always carried in the door pocket, in case he ran across a very aggressive snake or gator.

"Just as I stepped out of the truck, Tucker jumped out from behind a bush and rushed me, holding a big ol' knife. I fired the first shot in the air to try and scare him. But then I saw the look in his eyes. This whole business—the fights, the kidnapping and then us tying him to a tree for gator bait—was just too much. He had gone crazy!

"He growled like an animal and charged at me. I managed to fend him off, but he was as strong as two men. I fired at him, hoping to hit his knife arm. I didn't realize your uncle had loaded the gun with rat shot. As close as I was to him, some of those bullet-sized shotgun shells must have caught him in the chest and hit something vital. I tried to get him to talk, but he just coughed and spat up blood. He was dead when I put him in the truck. I'm sure he was involved in the kidnapping and the other stuff, but now we'll never be able to prove it." As an afterthought, Jimbo added, "I stopped on the way back at the quarter wash, to get the blood and dirt off of your uncle's truck."

Brad relaxed, and tried to think of an apology. However, admitting he thought Jimbo a conspirator, let alone the brains behind a plot to extort money from his uncle, would undoubtedly break any bond between them. Jimbo's simple trust and loyalty deserved better.

"I know you was upset about me not finding out where

your uncle is and I'm sorry, I truly am. But he's still alive, I can feel it."

It was torturing Brad to see Jimbo so torn apart. Still, he found it difficult to know what to say without making things worse. Finally, hoping his voice didn't quiver, Brad asked, "What did they say the weather's going to be like tomorrow?"

Jimbo's face brightened as he repeated the weather forecast and tried to speculate about its effect on the fishing.

Brad said, starting on another tack, "Say, Jimbo, do the names Frank du Boise and Harley Deer Corporation mean anything to you?"

Jimbo screwed up his face as if the effort to search his mind was painful. "Can't say I recall anything about that Deer Corporation, but Frank du Boise was the sheriff's father. Passed away a couple years back. Say, are you all right?" he asked. The color had drained out of Brad's face.

Brad felt like he'd been punched in the stomach, but he answered, "I'm fine, just a little stressed out. I think I'll have a beer."

Brad nursed his beer and tried to relax. He preferred a glass of wine, but he thought any port in a storm would have to do. He still didn't fully understand the implications of this piece of information. So the sheriff owned the property next to his uncle's. He wondered if it could have anything to do with her visit to the bank this morning, or for that matter, with the kidnapping of his uncle.

That's when the telephone rang. Brad picked it up, and was just about to say hello when a voice said, "Just listen! On Sunday, after the fishing tournament weigh-in is over, put a Styrofoam cooler with $150,000 in unmarked bills under the stage at the end nearest the dumpster. You will receive another call one hour later, telling you the location of George Allen. Remember, if anything goes wrong, you'll never see your uncle alive again." A click and a dial tone ended the one-sided conversation.

Brad asked Jimbo if the tournament would still be held without his uncle's presence. Jimbo informed him that George actually had very little to do with the tournament. A tournament committee was formed to start the contest on each day, check the boats in at the end of eight hours and supervise the weigh-in. George would say a few words of welcome before the start of the tournament, and award the first place prize to the winner on Sunday. Volunteers from among the families of employees would help with serving food, drinks, checking live-wells and releasing the fish after the weigh-in.

Brad told Jimbo about the phone call regarding the ransom money, and about his mixed feelings concerning the sheriff. It unnerved Brad slightly that Jimbo never pried. Jimbo, on the other hand, always figured people would tell him what they wanted him to know. It's not that he wasn't curious, it was just that he was a very private person and he respected other people's privacy. Finally, Brad related what he had learned at the courthouse regarding the ownership of the property adjoining his uncle's, or his, boat factory. In his eyes, it mattered very little. What mattered was, they were no closer to finding Uncle George or those responsible for the attacks, the bomb or the kidnapping than they were when they started. In fact, Brad told Jimbo they were probably one step back now, since the one man they felt sure was involved was now dead.

He admitted to himself that he was not very good at organizing or analyzing clues or facts. If the sheriff was unable to get to the bottom of this, he'd be pretty arrogant to think that he could. Unless of course, the sheriff was involved. It seemed perfectly obvious that somebody wanted his uncle's land or money or both. His uncle and the bank president had both mentioned offers from corporate interests to buy the business, and a corporation owned all of the property in the cove except his uncle's and the sheriffs. Brad came to a decision.

He said to Jimbo, "The way I see it, there are only two things I can do. One is to see if Pat will have dinner with me, now that I know she owns the land next to mine, and find out if she has had any offers. The other is to call the bank and borrow the money, using the property as collateral, then play it by ear and follow the kidnappers' demands."

He had given it considerable thought. Had it been a movie script, there would be obvious clues, a roomful of suspects, and, regardless how convoluted a plot, it would be brought to a successful conclusion in under three hours. But this was real life. Nothing was black or white. Everything and everybody involved was painted in various shades of gray.

"By the way," he continued, "while I'm taking care of business, pull Uncle George's old bass boat out of the water and transfer what gear we'll need for the tournament to the fancy rig in the garage. And check everything out. If everything goes smoothly, I'll meet you there tomorrow, in the early afternoon. I'm sure it looks terribly cold-hearted, but I know Uncle George wanted me to fish this tournament, and that matters to me."

Jimbo didn't think it was cold-hearted at all, and he agreed with Brad completely. Putting his arm around Brad's shoulder and gripping him warmly, Jimbo walked out the door.

Minutes later, Brad looked at his watch. The term

"banker's hours" added a sense of urgency to his telephone call to Reed Hadley. Yes, he was in and yes, he would prepare the necessary documents, and in fact, he could have the money in cash by tomorrow afternoon. That was easy, Brad thought. Almost too easy.

His next call was to Sheriff Patricia du Boise. Somewhat reluctantly, she agreed to have dinner with him, insisting on preparing dinner at her house. He was getting strange vibes from her. First, uncontrollable desire and passion, followed immediately by cold indifference. Then aloof, almost distrustful or suspicious. In truth, similar feelings about her had gone through his mind. Getting directions to her house, he hung up.

Now, he needed to find his way to one of the liquor stores Jimbo had shown him. He hoped one would have packaged goods other than beer and whiskey. This evening called for a bottle of his favorite, Beringer White Zinfandel.

His college friends had fondly referred to him as "the fruity guy who liked that sissy drink." But he knew his friends drank for the sole purpose of getting drunk and on a college student's budget cheaper was better. In fact, he knew some genuine borderline alcoholics who were seldom seen without a brown bag wrapped around a bottle of some cheap wine. He, on the other hand, didn't like to feel out of control. And after experiencing intoxication once, he never felt the urge again.

He did, however, enjoy the light, fruity flavor of a good zinfandel. The sensation of flavors mixing between good wine and good food made his mouth come alive, and greatly increased his enjoyment of a meal. He guessed he was at a rather low level of sophistication, as he could never really enjoy the drier, heavier-bodied wines. Maybe it had to do with the names, which he couldn't pronounce.

Even by itself, white zinfandel is a pleasant-tasting alcoholic beverage, and an interesting conversation piece, not to mention a quick way to get into a bar fight.

The first place he went only carried whiskey and beer. It even had cold beer singles in display coolers, but no white zinfandel. The friendly clerk, who was about his own age, suggested he go across the street to the drug store, which turned out to have exactly what he was looking for on sale.

Leaving the drugstore with a bag cradled in his arm containing several bottles, Brad noticed the sky had become cloudy and the wind had picked up. The air felt considerably cooler, and had all the indications of an approaching cold front. Just the thing to set the fishing back twenty-four to forty-eight hours.

It was just as he suspected, a frontal system. Brad knew a lot about post-frontal bass fishing. These fronts usually appeared every couple of days during prime fishing season. They pushed some rain or thunderstorms in front of cooler weather, followed by cloudless sunny skies. Some experts claimed that the rapidly dropping, then rapidly rising atmospheric pressure made it difficult for bass to maintain their internal balance, causing them to suspend at certain depths and be ambivalent feeders. Others maintained that the high bluebird skies' strong light penetration hurt the bass's eyes. Experts have reported seeing fish, their noses tucked deep into underwater grass, with only their tails showing, paying no attention to the offerings of fishermen. But no matter the cause, the resulting description of the fishing is usually "slow," which means no fish have been caught in the last twenty-four hours. The reason all fishermen don't just sit home after the passage of a cold front and stare at their clocks is that there's always a chance for aggressive fish, who seem unaware of the rules regarding frontal systems. As the sinking sun streaked the gathering clouds, painting them a veritable rainbow of colors, Brad tried to remember the Navy poem. "Red sky in the evening . . . " No! "Red sky in the morning, sailors take warning . . . "

Nearly passing the street which Pat told him to turn onto, Brad forced his thoughts back to his present dilemma. The mobile home he pulled up to had a late-model car in the driveway with a logo above the word "Sheriff." It was a double-wide trailer, with an aluminum skirt around its base and a peaked roof that resembled that of a real house. The postage-stamp-sized square of grass, with its flower border, almost completely hid the concrete pad the home sat upon. All in all, it looked much nicer than most of the others he had driven past.

After ringing the doorbell, and a brief pause, Pat opened the door. Her appearance was the biggest surprise of Brad's evening. She was dressed in a white blouse and red shorts. The blouse had a low neckline and unbuttoned just enough to hint of her considerable charms. The red shorts looked as if they were sprayed on. She blushed heavily from the expression Brad couldn't contain.

"Is something the matter?" Pat cooed.

It was Brad's turn to blush, not realizing it was so obvious. "Why, you're . . . you're positively a vision! You're the most beautiful woman I've ever seen in my life . . . I'm sorry, that just slipped out."

This won't do, Pat thought to herself, completely flustered. *He's hardly in the door, and in two more minutes we'll be tearing each other's clothes off.*

Clearing her throat, she said, "So nice of you to come over. This town suffers horribly from a lack of good restaurants. I'm really a pretty good cook."

Brad responded, relieved that she had changed the

subject. "I'm glad you invited me over. There are several things I'd like to discuss with you, and a crowded restaurant isn't quite the right place. I brought some wine. I wasn't sure if you drank wine, or even if it will go with what you've prepared, but . . . Do you have something to open the bottle with? I could use a drink!"

"Sure," she chuckled, under control again. "Look in the drawer next to the kitchen sink. The glasses are in the cabinet above. We can sit and talk a while in the living room while we have our wine."

Pat's kitchen wasn't at all what he expected. He thought it would be severely cramped, with tiny appliances. Past the kitchen, he saw a bathroom and a bedroom beyond that, and he assumed another bedroom with possibly a second bath on the other end beyond the living room. The home was neat and tastefully furnished.

He found the corkscrew, and opened the bottle easily. Looking in the upper cabinet, he found the wineglasses. Life was just full of surprises. He carried the bottle and the glasses into the living room, set them on a coffee table, and sat in the empty twin of the chair Pat was sitting on. He noticed she didn't sit on the couch. He thought it was probably a good thing, considering his feverish thoughts and raging hormones. He filled the glasses, taking the first and performing the ritual sniffing and sampling before handing one to her.

She took it all in, then asked, "What is it you want to discuss with me?"

Brad grimaced, "I'm not very good at guessing games, nor do I enjoy playing the fool."

Pat looked puzzled, "I don't understand."

Brad tried again, "Maybe I'm just naive, but I thought there was some chemistry between us. Maybe it's only me. I thought at first we both felt it. Perhaps I was feeling enough for the two of us."

Pat stared at him a long time, then said, "There is . . . or was, until I talked to Reed Hadley at the bank."

"Now, I'm beginning to understand. What did he tell you about me?"

She answered hotly, "He told me why you've been playing up to me. He told me all you cared about was getting me to sell you my property in the cove, so that you and your uncle could make a huge profit reselling it to some large corporation that wants to build a casino and hotel."

So that was it. Now he understood why Pat had suddenly become so cold. His instinctive dislike of Reed Hadley blinded him to his real purpose. "And you believed him?"

"Not at first. But yesterday, he showed me papers he was preparing for you to borrow enough money to buy up the cove property," she sniffed.

Brad realized that he had drastically underestimated Hadley's foresight. Taking the sheriff's mind off of her job and giving her reason to doubt the Allens' integrity certainly would give her pause to question his motives. *But why?* he thought to himself.

"Would you believe me if I told you that until this morning, I didn't know you owned the property next to my uncle's? Hell, until then, I didn't even know your last name!" Brad exclaimed, going on to tell her about his trip to the courthouse and his transaction at the bank.

She narrowed her eyes and said, "If what you say is true, then Reed Hadley is lying. And if he is, he could very well end up with your land and the money. And if he's linked to the Harley Deer Corporation, only my lot would stand between them and ownership of the entire cove."

"But what proof do we have?" Brad asked her, dejectedly.

Her thoughts busy and unhearing, she continued, "He's asked me to marry him several times. If I said yes, he'd own the entire cove. I've been such a fool!"

She set her glass on the table and, leaning over to take Brad's in mid-drink, she set his down next to hers. The questioning look on his face and the words accompanying it were cut short as she threw herself on top of him, her lips locked on his, her tongue exploring his mouth. As they toppled to the floor, hands on buttons and zippers, breath coming in gasps, shoes bouncing on the floor and sweat covering their bodies, they paid no heed to the buzzer, which indicated that the food in the oven was ready to eat.

A good deal later, sitting at the kitchen table, dressed only in undergarments and eating the overcooked food, Brad couldn't help but think it was the best meal he'd ever had.

"I'm sorry about the food," Pat whispered, her eyes half closed. "I'll do better next time."

"The food was fine," Brad replied, suppressing a yawn. "And I thought you did it perfect this time."

They both giggled like school children discovering a forbidden body part for the first time.

"And now for dessert," Pat sang, as she took his hand and led him to the bedroom.

8

Brad awoke to the flash of lightning and the sound of thunder. He tried to jump up, but found his right arm pinned beneath a heavy weight. The heavy weight turned out to be Pat. She certainly wasn't heavy, he reconsidered, gazing at her naked body draped in blissful slumber over his arm, with one of her legs wrapped around one of his. He lay back down and listened to the rain spatter on the tin roof of the mobile home.

The next time he came back to consciousness, Pat was gone. Sitting up in the severely rumpled bed, he heard the sounds of dishes clattering and melodic singing coming from the kitchen. The tune played by the continuing rainfall seemed in harmony with her lilting song. The faint sound of a radio or television added to the musical symmetry. He got slowly out of the bed and looked about the room. His memory went back to the evening's activities. *My God*, he thought, they were at each other most of the night. *That ought to hold you for a while*, he told himself. But even the very thought brought back faint stirrings of desire. "You animal," he whispered aloud, and went looking for the shower.

Afterward, Brad, freshly clean, sat at the kitchen table, letting the last drops of coffee slide down his throat. He watched Pat, dressed only in an extra large T-shirt, bounce about the kitchen as she cleared the remains of the eggs Benedict and bananas Foster from the table. She quickly rinsed the dishes, loaded them in the dishwasher, sat down at the table and refilled their coffee cups. The hot liquid explored his stomach as he stretched his legs out and patted his considerably full abdomen. "You not only look good, but you cook good, too," he said, trying to tickle her bare feet with his toes. "You learn how to cook from your mother?"

"I hardly knew my mother," she replied. "She died when I was very young. My father raised me, mostly by himself. He was about as Cajun as they get. He taught me to cook, among other things. It was really because of him that I ran for the job of sheriff."

"But Jimbo told me your father died several years ago," Brad offered.

"Actually, it was just two years ago when they found his boat, after it drifted up to an old dock. The weather had been mild, there was plenty of gas in the engine, and all of his fishing gear was intact. Several days later, his body washed up, but by then it wasn't a pretty sight. The toothy critters in the Bend aren't too particular what they eat. I might have dismissed it as an ordinary drowning if it hadn't been for two things."

"And they were? . . ."

"First of all, he worked most of his life on the water. He used to pilot a supply craft between the offshore oil rigs and the mainland. He was always safety-conscious. Never took his life jacket off until he got off the water. They found his life vest in the boat.

"Secondly, the autopsy showed enough alcohol in his blood to make him legally drunk. I never knew him to take so much as one beer with him while he was driving his boat. He always said that alcohol and water didn't mix! The medical examiner called it accidental drowning. I ran for sheriff to prove otherwise. It's been two whole years, and I haven't found one piece of evidence to the contrary."

Brad thought about what she said, the silence heavy in the air, until he said, "Seems to me, someone's very, very good at causing accidents. The parallels between my uncle's accidents and your father's are far too many to be simple coincidence."

"I hadn't thought of that," she said, wrinkling her brow as she considered his words.

"In fact," he continued, "now that I hear your story, I have more reason to believe my uncle is still alive! Tucker Jones didn't have time to do away with Uncle George before we . . . well, I just don't think he had enough time. And Jimbo killed him in self-defense before he could get back to finish the job. I just hope the person behind Tucker doesn't know where he took Uncle George. I'd bet good money Reed Hadley is behind everything. But proving it is another matter."

She agreed, then asked Brad what his next move would be.

"Well, I'm to pick up the money this afternoon. I'd like you to keep it for me until Sunday. After the tournament weigh-in, I'll explain how it's to be delivered. I know it sounds terribly cold and heartless of me to even think about the tournament, let alone fish in it. But I also can't see how sitting in the house, staring at the phone and worrying will do any good. Besides, the tournament is very important to my uncle. Alive or dead, he'd want me to be in it."

Pat assured him she would do everything in her power to help find his uncle while he fished the tournament. And maybe, she thought, find some answers concerning her father's death at the same time.

Preparing to go, Brad told Pat his plans: he had to purchase a plain Styrofoam cooler, meet Jimbo and attend the evening meeting at the marina. He also thought it best if they weren't seen together any more than necessary, so they didn't make the kidnappers nervous. He also mentioned his need for rest from his night's exertions.

She pouted and struck a sensual pose as he headed for the door. He stepped out into the persistent rain, the screen door separating them as she pressed her voluptuous body against the screen.

"You're going to get soaking wet," she giggled as he stood, ignoring the drops running down his face.

Blowing her a kiss, he said, "I need a cold shower!" Then, he walked to his truck.

The rain turned to a foggy mist as Brad turned back toward town. Suppressing a shudder, he tried to assess his feelings toward Pat. Definite magnetic attraction, real physical and emotional compatibility, lust without a doubt, but love? He surprised himself that he could describe his relationship with Pat and not use the word love. It bewildered him to think that only last week he didn't believe in recreational sex. The word "gray" seemed to come to mind.

He passed the bank, the sheriff s office and the courthouse. Another mile down the road, he turned into the parking lot of the Big Bend Discount Farm Store. He parked in the closest available space, but walking in the rain, it felt like a mile away. He hurried to the door which slid noiselessly to the side. Where the handle should have been was a sticker which read, "In an emergency, pushing here will cause the door to swing open." He wondered why the door couldn't swing open without it being an emergency.

The store not belonging to one of the major chains, Brad could only guess the whereabouts of the sporting goods department. To his surprise, large red signs hanging from the ceiling directed him to the proper area, and one aisle over, he found what he was looking for. According to the sign on the shelf below, the larger size cooler was on sale for less than the price of the smaller sized one. He chose the one on sale, as it looked large enough to hold the ransom money, although he really had no idea how big a pile one hundred and fifty thousand dollars would make.

He carried it to the front of the store, thinking of coming back sometime just to browse the aisles. He loved looking at the multitude of strange-looking objects occupying the shelves in the farm section, and trying to guess their functions. It never ceased to impress him with the apparent quality and simplicity of work clothes and farm tools. One thing however, which reminded him of discount stores at home, was the many rows of registers, yet only one with a checkout person looking harried by the long line of disgruntled customers.

Finally getting to the counter, he put the cooler down and reached for his wallet. The second thing that reminded him of home was the adolescent girl behind the counter with the bad complexion, chewed fingernails, pink paint sprayed on the bird's nest she called a hairdo, and the bad attitude. The smile on her lips bore no relationship to the shape of her mouth and the insincere "How are you today?" fit her perfectly. She aimed a scan tool at the bar code sticker on the side, and when nothing happened, she repeated the action several times. She then keyed in the numbers at the bottom. Still nothing.

"Maybe this will help," Brad suggested, turning the cooler over exposing a tag marked "sale." The original price had been crossed out, leaving "$2.59" neatly printed in ink.

The girl told him that while that might indeed be the price, she could not ring it up unless the computer recognized the item and showed the correct cost. But not exactly in those words. For what seemed like several minutes, the girl looked from the register to the cooler and back again, as if hoping for some miracle to occur, and register the right price. Out of patience, Brad was about to say something insulting when a man appeared and assaulted the keyboard with flying fingers. He wore a white shirt with a red bow tie and had an impressive collection of pencils and ball point pens in his pocket protector. "She's new here," he spewed out as the correct information appeared on the display. And as quickly as he had appeared, he was gone. Brad felt like saying, "Who was that masked man?" but he thought the sarcasm would be wasted on the girl.

He handed her a five-dollar bill and prayed that the power didn't fail before she figured out how much change to give him. He put the money in his pocket, picked up the cooler and headed out, pausing only to say, "No thanks, I don't want it in a sack."

As he neared the exit door, Brad heard the fading refrain of "Have a nice day" echo in his ears. He only broke stride long enough to make sure the automatic door knew this was not an emergency, and that he would not have to push it open to save his nose.

The fog was settling in. Brad had to turn on his headlights as he retraced his route to the bank. True to his word, Reed Hadley had prepared all of the necessary documents for Brad to sign. An assistant manager, who was also Hadley's secretary, handed Brad the triplicate papers, some with names he had never heard before. As he signed each one, he hoped all he stood to lose was a piece of property that, until a few days ago, he didn't even know he had. When he had signed all of them, Hadley's assistant removed the bottom copy of each document, folded them neatly and put them in a brown packet.

"These are your copies," she said dryly, glaring at him over the half-glasses she wore far down on her prominent nose. She excused herself and walked into the vault. She returned carrying a canvas bag. She opened it, reached inside and brought out banded bundles of bills, stacking them neatly on the desk in front of Brad.

"Count them, if you please," she said, as if the effort was causing her great pain. "If your count equals one hundred and fifty thousand dollars, please sign this receipt."

She laid a form down next to the pile of money. It was also in triplicate. Brad took his time counting the money. When he finished, he signed the receipt. She tore the third copy, and inserted it into the envelope.

"You may keep the satchel," she said indifferently. "Good day to you, Mr. Allen."

Brad put the bundles of money carefully back in the duffel, zipped it shut, lifted it by the handles, and walked out of the door.

It was less than a block to the sheriff's office, but Brad elected to drive as the fog was getting so thick, it was like a fine mist. He also wanted to give Pat every opportunity to get to the office. He felt his way through the parking lot to the rear entrance, although he was pretty sure no one could have seen him, as he could barely see the gym bag he was carrying.

Pat was sitting in her office, tapping a pencil on her desk and staring sightlessly into space. Brad's knock on the door broke her reverie. He walked in and dropped the canvas bag on her desk.

"I assume that's the money," she stated matter-of-factly, not bothering to look inside. Brad nodded. "I'll put it in the safe. I'm the only one who has the combination."

Brad told her about the telephone call and the Styrofoam cooler. She agreed to get the money to him at the appointed time without drawing attention. He thanked her again, made his way back to his truck, and drove out of town.

The headlight beams reflected off of the thick fog. Brad could no longer see the center line of the road, so he slowed to a crawl and hugged the edge of the pavement with his emergency flashers blinking. He figured the fog would be heavier closer to the water, as the water by this time was warmer than the air. He hoped for a land breeze to blow the fog away, or for sunshine to follow the passing cold front and burn it off. But as the road climbed to the higher shoreline, the fog actually began to dissipate and, before long, he spotted the driveway leading to the garage.

The sight of the rubble from the burned-out boat factory gripped Brad's stomach like a vise. He saw Jimbo's old pickup truck at the top of the boat ramp, with Uncle George's first boat safely bunked on its trailer, hitched to the rear bumper. Water was still dripping from the livewell drain. Brad assumed Jimbo had recently pulled it from the water and was now in the process of unloading the gear. He brought their equipment into the garage, and put it in the fancy experimental rig they would use the next day.

Brad entered the garage through the service door, and saw Jimbo sorting through the mountain of fishing and boating equipment. Jimbo responded to Brad's appearance with a nod and went back to his task.

Without looking up, Jimbo said, "You might as well sort through the pile of rods and reels and choose the ones you'll want to use in the tournament. Mine are already in the boat. Your uncle designed everything a fisherman could possibly want into this boat. Price was no object. But it's strictly a concept rig, not in the least cost-effective. Not yet, anyway."

Brad noticed a full-length rod storage compartment at the front of the aft casting deck. He walked over to the assortment of tackle and after a few minutes' thought, selected six outfits, which he carried to the boat.

"On the wall back of the workbench, you'll find most every kind and weight of line, and an automatic line winder. You might want to strip those reels and restring them."

Brad selected twenty-pound monofilament line for the five bait-casting reels and ten-pound for the one spinning reel. For two of the bait-casting reels, he chose a high visibility line, plus one low visibility line for the other three. Not knowing what water clarity or fish mood they would encounter, he wanted to be prepared for any eventuality. Jimbo glanced at him from time to time, nodding his approval.

As Brad was finishing the last reel, Jimbo looked up and said, "Look over these lures. If you don't see what you want to use, just ask me. We've got what you want here somewhere."

For the spinning rod, Brad found a quarter-ounce bullet weight and a wide gap hook, to rig Texas-style if the wind was calm and the fishing was slow. On the seven-foot medium heavy flipping rod, he tied a seven-sixteenths-ounce black rattle jig, dressed with a plastic three-inch frog, his "confidence lure." On another seven-footer, he made up a Carolina rig with a two-foot leader and a three-quarter-ounce egg sinker. This he tipped with a pumpkin, watermelon French fry.

Unlike the majority of the rods, one was not graphite. Instead, it was an E-glass composite, also seven feet long, but more suitable for use with crank baits. For this, he chose a deep-diving, lipped crank bait in a natural bass color. Of the two six-foot-six inch rods, one was rigged with a half-ounce, double-willow leaf spinner bait with a chartreuse skirt. Since the water was usually slightly stained, the other was a lipless crank bait with built-in rattles. This he could rip through underwater grass beds to attract fish buried deep in the foliage.

Jimbo watched as Brad tied each knot, tied to complement the particular lure he used on each rod. He was impressed by Brad's lure selection and knot-tying expertise. Jimbo was delighted that Brad had figured out the possible conditions they could expect in the tournament during the two days they spent pre-fishing. This boy was no greenhorn, Jimbo thought.

By the time they had finished stowing all the fishing rods, life jackets, extra lures, rain gear and spare parts, tested all of the electronics, filled the gas tank and the oil injection reservoir, they would barely have time to grab some supper before their meeting at the marina. Jimbo suggested a quick bite at the marina's snack shop to save time and travel.

"Besides," he explained, "Good nutrition and bass fishing don't seem to go together. Why, during one tournament, I lived on beef jerky and coffee, three meals a day for three days. One local guide who used to work around here would meet his customers at the breakfast joint in town. One morning, he showed up right from an all-night bender, ordered a plate full of biscuits and gravy, topped with two strips of bacon, covered with two eggs sunny-side-up and two slices of cheese. He commenced to clean the plate, wash it down with three cups of Boston coffee loaded with sugar. Then he took his party out and fished for eight hours, came in, cleaned fish, took a shower and went back out drinking. And he never once worried about nutrition!"

"I suppose you're going to tell me he's healthy as a horse," Brad interjected.

"Nope," Jimbo snipped, "He's dead as a doornail!"

Those were the most words Brad had ever heard Jimbo say all at one time, and he stared at him in wonder.

The snack bar was just what the name implied. The cold cases were stocked with juices, soft drinks, beer and bottled water. Shelving units and hanging displays held every type of munchy imaginable, several styles of jerky, not to mention pickled eggs and hocks. So much for health foods, Brad thought. Behind a counter, beneath a heat lamp were trays of French fries, fried chicken parts, hamburgers and hot dogs. A sign on the glass front read "Cold Sandwiches Available." Brad wondered if that's what they did with the hot foods at the end of the day. A heavy-set, middle-aged woman, sweating profusely, stood ready to take their order.

Jimbo ordered a chicken basket, which contained five unrecognizable chicken parts and lots of soggy fries. A tiny paper cup filled with either coleslaw or tartar sauce and a rock-hard dinner roll completed the chicken dinner special.

The sweaty lady commented disinterestedly, "Napkins and plastic utensils are over by the wall. Catsup and mustard's on the table."

Brad decided on a hot dog with a bag of potato chips, then added, "I'll pay for the food. Get whatever you want to drink, and if you don't mind, bring me a Coke."

To Brad, only one thing was worse than sitting at a greasy table: sitting at a greasy table with a short leg. He finally got tired of their drinks slopping out of the can every time they tried to spear a French fry or rest an elbow, so he folded several napkins and wedged them under the offending leg.

They ate in silent contemplation until Brad broke the hush. "Well, is it coleslaw or tartar sauce?"

Jimbo purposefully took another spoonful before responding. "I really can't tell."

The meeting took place at the side of the marina, in front of a permanent stage with a leader board nailed between two badly weathered wooden uprights. The entire stage looked neglected and questionably fragile. A man walked to the middle of the platform, carrying what appeared to be a microphone, and unrolled a well-worn cord.

Jimbo seemed to know everybody as they milled through the growing crowd. Brad lost track of the names that went along with the hands he shook.

Jimbo leaned close to Brad's ear and said, "We're expecting about a hundred boats or two hundred people, give or take a few. One of the team must own a Caliente boat or be an employee of the company. All of the entry fees are used for prizes. Your uncle is paying all other expenses. It's his way of thanking people for their loyalty."

Brad looked at his watch. It was ten minutes after seven, and he could sense the restlessness of the crowd. Finally, a tall, thin, well-dressed man mounted the stage and bent over to pick up the microphone. Brad was taken aback as he recognized Reed Hadley. He began by welcoming everyone, and thanking them for coming. He then launched into the recitation of the rules and regulations of the tournament.

Due to the number of boats entered, it was decided that there would be four flights, ten minutes apart. The times would be adjusted according to which flight each contestant was on. Each flight of approximately twenty-five boats would take off in a shotgun start. The first flight was to leave at first light. The flights reversed on the second day.

Hadley read off the list of prizes, then asked if anyone had a question about any of the rules. Next, the manager of the marina explained the launching procedure, and informed the group where to park their vehicles and boat trailers.

Finally, taking the microphone again, Hadley asked Brad to say a few words in his uncle's absence. Brad climbed to the stage, planks creaking beneath his feet as he walked to the center and took the microphone from Reed Hadley.

"I've already had the pleasure of meeting some of you. My name is Brad Allen, George Allen's nephew. As most of you probably know by now, my uncle has been kidnapped." A hush went through the crowd. Brad noticed several men jab one another with an elbow. "George Allen put his boat company before all else in his life. He realized that any success he had was due in great part to his employees, whom he also considered his friends. Even when his factory, his dream and his life's work was destroyed, his thoughts were not of himself, but of the men and women who helped make his dream come true." As he spoke, he glanced at Reed Hadley's face, which was void of any expression. "He even brought me down here to help me get my life together. The success of this tournament meant more to him than the danger he was being threatened with. I hope as you all enjoy the next two days of fishing in the spirit of competition and sportsmanship, you will take a moment to say a prayer for George Allen's safe return. Jimbo and I will be fishing in his place, and we both wish each and every one of you good luck and good fishing!"

The crowd reacted as one. They clapped their hands and stamped their feet, whistling and cheering and patting one another on the back. Brad fought back tears as he jumped down off the stage.

Jimbo clasped him in a bearlike embrace and said, "Once you get wound up, you really know how to work a crowd! Your uncle would be mighty proud of you. There wasn't a dry eye in the house."

"Except for Reed Hadley."

9

Brad tossed and turned that night, trying every trick and relaxation technique to get the sleep that continued to elude him. He heard Jimbo's even snoring coming from the next room. He stared at the red glow of the digital clock on the nightstand, trying not to count the blinks of the cursor. But sixty seconds made a minute, and minutes built into hours. His mind raced, first to his uncle's whereabouts, then to the tournament, and finally to Pat, only to start over again. He wasn't sure exactly when sleep overtook him, but the next thing he knew, Jimbo was shaking him gently.

"I think it's time we get started. I've been giving it some thought, and since we're so close to the factory, uh, garage, you know what I mean, we can save time by launching from there and running to the marina. I've looked outside, and the moon is full and bright. Not a cloud in the sky."

Brad agreed, and got up to dress. As he hopped around the room trying to get a shoe on his foot, Jimbo said, "I've also got a thermos of hot coffee on the kitchen counter."

Brad thought again of his uncle. With Jimbo around, there wouldn't be much more a wife could do.

As usual, Jimbo was right. In minutes they were backed up to the garage. Jimbo went in through the service door to unlock and open the large overhead door, so Brad could back in and hook up the waiting boat and trailer. That being accomplished, Brad pulled out of the open door, and backed the rig straight down the ramp to the water. Meanwhile, Jimbo was behind the wheel of the boat, preparing to start the engine as soon as it hit the water. Brad rode the brake, inching back until he heard the throaty roar of the highly tuned motor. He paused for several minutes, as the popping and spitting smoothed to a steady rumble. Through the rearview mirror, he saw the combined boat and truck exhaust separate as Jimbo maneuvered the boat off the partially submerged trailer and away from the ramp. He quickly put the truck in drive and pulled up to the garage, so he could close and lock the doors on his way to the boat dock. Jimbo was waiting there, holding onto a cleat to keep from drifting away.

Brad stepped from the dock to the rear casting deck, pausing long enough to remove the life jacket from the rear butt-seat and put it on while climbing in next to Jimbo, who turned on the running lights, shifted into gear, and idled toward the mouth of the cove.

The predawn air, cool and humid, caused droplets of moisture to drip from Brad's nose and chin as they glided along the mirrored surface on full plane. An occasional bug, unlucky enough to get in the way, made a splatting noise on the windshield, which was streaked with fog and condensation. In the light of the full moon, Brad could see the shimmering reflection of the hull, riding only on its small planing pad and the motor's lower unit. The large boat lane buoys flew by as Brad turned his head, trying to read the speedometer.

Not taking his eyes from the direction they were heading, Jimbo yelled, "Don't worry, we're not even at half throttle! If the wind stays down come daylight, you'll see this thing fly!"

The engine's hum kept constant as Jimbo followed the

curving shoreline, not bothering to slow down as they went into the turn. Brad could feel the turning hooks bite and hold as the hull tracked with negligible side slip. Ahead, he could see running lights, red and green bow and white stern, of other boats. Jimbo backed off the throttle, turned out of the boat lane, and picked up the iridescent glow of small markers leading to the marina. Rounding a wooded point, Brad saw the launch ramp lights, plus a long line of headlights and taillights from cars and trailers in the midst of launching and parking. The area around the floating, covered boat stalls was crowded with bass boats drifting aimlessly, their running lights shining and engines idling.

Jimbo headed for the end of a floating dock, on which several people were standing. "We need to have them check our live well to make sure we haven't brought our fish with us, and pull a number from a hat which will tell us what flight we're in."

For all his experience, Brad had not fished many tournaments and he was fascinated by the flurry of activity. "I suppose this is more organized than it looks," Brad remarked.

Jimbo replied, "Now, you can see why I suggested we run here rather than fight the crowd. It will be worse at the end of the day."

Number "36" put them in the second flight, so Jimbo idled to the middle of the pack, shut off the main engine and put down the trolling motor to control their drift and keep them from bumping into other boats.

"After the first flight goes off, we'll move toward the front so we can get some clean water for our turn," Jimbo said.

The first rays of sunlight streaked the horizon as the voice from the loudspeaker drowned out the sound of the lapping wavelets and spitting engines. "Your attention, please. It is now six o'clock. Flight number one will be due back no later than two p.m. Gentlemen, start your engines!"

The announcement was followed immediately by the shot of a starters pistol. Twenty-five high-powered bass boats pulled hole shots, maneuvering to avoid the wakes and waves of others as they made for the boat lanes, some going north, others heading south. Brad and Jimbo held fast to the handrails as their boat pitched and rolled from the backwash of the speeding boats.

Wiping droplets of spray from his face, Brad said, "I assume you have a plan."

Jimbo replied, "Remember where we left Tucker Jones? Well, the undercut banks and rushes can provide good cover for bass if they're holding because of the weather conditions we've had. You can flip your jig and pig and I'll try a top water along the edges. Then we'll see what the sky looks like as the sun comes up."

Jimbo pulled back the sleeve of his jacket, and looked at the illuminated gauges of his watch. He folded the trolling motor onto its cradle and climbed behind the wheel, hooking the lanyard from the dead man's switch to his life vest. He started the engine as the voice once again pierced the air. "Flight number two, it is now 6:10 a.m. You are due back no later than 2:10 p.m.." Again, the announcement was followed by the bark of the starter's pistol. Jimbo hammered the throttle down. The engine instantly began to produce a deep-throated roar. The front of the boat jerked up, obscuring Brad's view. The force of acceleration drained the blood from his face, leaving him slightly lightheaded. As Jimbo trimmed the engine up, the boat came onto plane, and its speed increased. Brad looked back through the rooster tail thrown up by the screaming engine, and saw the other boats far behind. Jimbo pulled back on the throttle.

"I don't think we need to go over a hundred miles an hour," he said, offhandedly. Brad pretended to check his underwear.

Leaving the main boat lane, Jimbo turned into a tree-choked cove. He hugged the shoreline, indicating he was following the old creek channel, then turned and began winding his way through the trees. Once they were in the midst of them, Brad could see the lane formed by the lines of trees which once arched over the meandering creek. Dropping their leaves into the mud-stained water, they were now bare-branched reminders of man's ability to change the landscape to suit his needs.

As they neared the back of the cove, Jimbo shut down the engine, picked up his rod from the casting deck, and lowered the trolling motor into the water. At the same time, Brad selected his flipping rig and took his place on the rear casting deck. Jimbo ran the trolling motor at its lowest speed, positioning the boat so the light breeze and current would move them along. Only an occasional burst of the trolling motor was necessary to correct the boat's direction.

Jimbo cast his top water bait to the edges of the reeds and rushes emerging from the shallow water, which made gurgling sounds as he walked it back to the boat. Brad flipped his jig and pig to likely-looking places adjacent to the boat, let it drop, twitched it once or twice, then retrieved it.

Half an hour later, the sun peered over the tops of the lush, green trees along the shore. Oaks, cottonwoods and pecans turned or uncurled their leaves to feel the warmth radiating through the cloudless sky. Birds greeted the new day with their merry chirping. Now and then, a squirrel or rabbit could be seen picking its way along, looking for food or scurrying for cover. Soon, they saw a snake slither onto a fallen log to warm itself, and a gator bob silently to the surface, with only its eyes and cleated back visible. Already, an endless array of turtles lined up on partially submerged branches and logs, only to drop off into the water as the passing boat disturbed their reverie. But not a peck nor a strike did they feel. Nothing to cause their hearts to skip a beat and the adrenaline to course through their veins and heighten their senses.

Nearing the mouth of the cove, Jimbo set his rod down and poured two cups of coffee. Handing one to Brad, he said, "When you finish that, we'll try another spot. We've got all we're going to get in here."

It was nearly nine before Brad caught their first bass. And since it was less than fourteen inches long, he had to release it. Jimbo got bit one time. Fishing along a rip-rap breakwater, he got a tremendous strike on a spinner bait. He fought for a full five minutes before seeing a ten-pound catfish break the surface. After a Texas release, they idled around to the protected side and tried to regroup. It was frustrating but not surprising that the fish were turned off. They were on the high side of a passing cold front, under a cloudless sky with little or no wind. The only positive thing was that the rain brought rising water.

Jimbo unfolded his lake map and examined it closely. "This lake is too big to run to every possible spot. What we need is a place where we can find a little of everything. If we can't catch them there, we can't catch them. It's nothing to be ashamed of. I fished a tournament once with six hundred other fishermen. Only five boats weighed in fish. In another one, one fish won everything, including biggest fish.

"But I know of one place. You can only get in there when the lake level is up. But it's got deep water, emerging vegetation a grassy shoreline, a large shallow flat and trees, of course. There's a narrow opening in a bluff wall. More like a gap, actually. But unless the water is up, you can't make it through the gap."

As they ran for Jimbo's secret spot, Brad took some time to appreciate the fine qualities of his uncle's experimental boat. Its ride and handling were phenomenal. Its speed and performance were outstanding. Plus, it looked sensational. The jury was still out, however, on its ability to lead to the big fish.

They slowed to an idle, raised the engine as high as it would go, still leaving the water pickup submerged, and inched their way through the gap. They entered what looked to Brad like an entirely different lake. In the distance, he saw several old houseboats. One was partially submerged, and listing badly to one side.

Jimbo saw him looking at them, and commented, "Those were mostly homemade. They were used for crappie fishing. Some were fixed up pretty fancy and had all the comforts of home. They could also be used as duck blinds by the hunters here about. But now, they're just rotting away. When they finally sink, they'll make good structure for bass. We can try fishing around them. Like boat docks, only out in the middle."

Brad stood up, shading his eyes and staring intently at the nearest boat. "It looks like someone's standing on that one and waving to us" Brad observed.

As they slowly approached the old houseboat, Brad's eyes got wider and wider, then filled with tears.

"I don't believe it," Jimbo repeated to himself, "I just don't believe it!"

"Hello, boys! Glad you could drop by. I've been getting

a mite hungry. All these bass around, and me with nothing I could use to catch them."

Brad and Jimbo cried in unison, "George!"

Brad grabbed an old rusted cleat, and looped a line around it to keep them from drifting. Then he ran to the front, and secured it there, also. Jimbo grabbed George in his viselike arms, lifting him bodily from the houseboat, and placing him on the deck gently.

George recounted the sum of his activities since his kidnapping between mouthfuls of snacks. Other than his rumpled clothing and growth of beard, he looked none the worse for wear.

"So, you don't actually know who brought you here."

George nodded his head at his nephew, still tearing at the plastic wrap enclosing the food Jimbo had brought along. "I was knocked unconscious," he said, touching the still-prominent knot on the back of his head. "When I woke up, it was dark and I was locked inside that houseboat. It's odd that no one ever came back to check on me."

Brad told him about Tucker Jones and the events leading to his demise. "If Tucker was your captor, that would explain why no one returned to check up on you. Although, my guess is if he had come back, it would have been to kill you."

Jimbo listened intently, nodding his head and patting George, as if he needed to touch him to prove to himself he was really alive and well. Suddenly, his hunger temporarily slaked, George looked around. His eyes took in the boat and the rods, each with their different lures, neatly laying on the deck. "The tournament! You're fishing in the tournament!"

"That's how we came to be here," Jimbo explained. "The bass have been mighty tight-tipped, and this place isn't well-known, except to the old timers."

Uncle George told them about the bass he saw around and under the houseboat.

"If you're sure you're all right, we might as well make a few casts and see if we can get bit," Brad offered.

Jimbo untied the bow line while Brad released the stern. Trying not to disturb the water, they let the breeze, such as it was, drift them away. Jimbo worked the trolling motor on its lowest speed, keeping the boat parallel to the houseboat. Brad flipped his jig and pig, letting it fall right off the corner of a weed-encrusted pontoon. George saw the line jump and was about to say so, when Brad cranked the reel slowly. He took the slack out of the line, lowered the rod tip and set the hook with a grunt. The rod tip stayed where it was, and the rod formed a curve back to the reel seat. Brad knew he was hooked up with a good fish.

"That's what we're here for!" he shouted excitedly, cranking the reel and pumping the madly jerking rod. Holding the rod high with his left hand, Brad dropped to his knees, lipped the wildly thrashing bass with his right, and heaved it into the boat.

"You won't have to measure that one," Uncle George said proudly.

Brad opened the live well, and lowered the fish into the aerated water.

Jimbo slowly retrieved his Texas-rigged plastic lizard, stopping, letting it fall, then reeling again. Another hook set shook the boat as Jimbo caught his first, a keeper. Its mouth distended by the lip hold, Jimbo handed the dripping green bass to George, who tossed it into the live well with its brother. Meanwhile, Jimbo moved them around to the other side of the houseboat. Two more casts netted them two more quality fish. One more keeper would give them their five-fish limit. They could then spend the remainder of their time culling, so as to increase the weight of their catch.

They moved from one houseboat to the next, but with no success. Whatever conditions caused bass to hold by the houseboat on which George Allen was held captive, evidently did not exist around the others.

Brad and Jimbo switched to spinner baits. They knew they could cover more water and fish faster, searching for aggressive bass. They moved along the shoreline, casting into the reeds and along the edges, but with no luck.

Jimbo looked at his watch. He gazed from Brad to George, trying to assess their feelings.

"I have a plan," he said. "I think we can assume the brains behind your uncle's kidnapping either don't know where he's at or think Tucker Jones killed him. In any case, they can't know we've found him. Let's drop him off at the garage before we weigh in. He can hide out there, and we can bring him food and whatever he needs. He'll have the advantage of being able to move about without being noticed. After the tournament, he can watch or follow whoever picks up the ransom money. Then we'll have 'em"

They all agreed the plan had merit, and even the little danger didn't sway George. "After all," he said, "if it weren't for you and Jimbo, I'd probably be dead anyway."

Jimbo started the engine and headed out through the gap. Once in deeper water, he steered for a boat lane.

"Now, let's see what this baby can really do!" Jimbo exclaimed as he slammed the throttle down, adjusting the trim as the boat got up on plane and picked up speed.

With no appreciable wind to add difficulty to their approach, they reached the dock in good time. George saw the remains of his factory as he stepped from the boat. Brad went through the motions of securing a bow and stern line, while Jimbo accompanied George to the garage.

Brad picked up his spinner-baited rod and began to fan cast from the rear deck. It was more to serve his nervous energy than any thought of actually catching a fish. Because of the conditions, he retrieved his lure using a slow roll, stopping to let the bait drop. Then, with a light jerk, he continued turning the crank.

On his third cast, he targeted a large tree trunk, half of which was growing out from the water. He hit the tree about a foot up from the surface, and let the spinner bait drop straight down along the root into the water. He paused until the ripples disappeared, then twitched the tip of his rod. The water erupted and the line moved to the side. Brad set the hook and reeled, stopping when he realized the fish was pulling his line against the drag.

He waited until the fish finished running, and started to pump and reel again. He made a little headway when the fish made another run. Keeping the rod tip down to prevent it from jumping and throwing the hook, he slowly felt it beginning to tire

He dropped to one knee, keeping the line tight, and brought the fish to the side of the boat. He reached down and grasped the lower jaw with the fingers of his hand. Up came a largemouth bass which, Brad estimated, weighed about eight pounds.

Brad's hand was still shaking and his heart still beat like a triphammer as Jimbo came walking back to the dock. Only his breathing returned to normal. Jimbo's pace picked up, becoming a full run as he saw the huge fish in Brad's grip.

"We're going to win, we're going to win!" Jimbo cried, landing in the boat without missing a stride. "Let's get weighed!"

Jimbo untied the boat and made ready to start the engine, while Brad added his trophy fish to the live well. They secured their gear, idled from the cove, and picked up the boat lane that would take them back to the marina.

"I told your uncle we'd bring him some food and clean clothes after the weigh-in," Jimbo yelled to Brad, trying to make his voice carry above the sound of the wind and the roar of the engine.

They arrived at the marina with minutes to spare, pulled up to the check-in dock, and reported their number. A judge asked if they had any fish to weigh. Brad's affirmative answer got him a plastic bag in which he was to put the fish. The judge added, "So far, I've only handed out three other bags."

Jimbo found an empty slip, tied the boat so the wind would keep it from bumping against the edge of the dock, while Brad reached into the live well five times, each time bringing out a fish. He put them all into the plastic bag and carried it to the stage, where two other judges emptied the contents into a plastic basket. The basket fit onto an electronic scale.

The crowd standing around the front of the platform let out a gasp as the read-out showed nineteen pounds, four ounces. Brad's big fish weighed slightly over eight pounds by itself. A judge neatly lettered their number at the top of the leader board and at the side, listed the eight-pounder at the top of the column marked "Largest Fish." If it held, it would be worth an extra thousand dollars. Brad watched as the fish were put into a large, water-filled stainless steel tank, where they were treated with chemicals to reduce shock. They would later be released without harm.

There were the usual questions, as a man with the

same worn microphone cable tried to get Brad to tell where he caught the fish and with what lure. Brad had seen enough tournaments to know better than to give that information on the first day of a two-day contest. He good-naturedly sidestepped the questions, leaving the stage with a big smile on his face.

Brad and Jimbo mixed with the crowd, talking fishing with people Jimbo had introduced Brad to earlier. They declined several offers of beers. After the last boat checked in, they remained in the lead by over four pounds.

While it was still daylight, and for the first time feeling no sense of urgency, they motored back to the garage. Brad gazed up at the sun, just beginning to color the thin wispy clouds forming in the early evening.

What little wind there was had died out, and the surface of the lake reflected the land and the sky like a mirror. The boat skimmed the flat water so smoothly, Brad thought he could easily confuse the two. With less throttle, the engine hummed a pleasant tune. The sound carried away from them, making it possible to carry on a conversation at normal volume. "We'll tie the boat at the dock," Jimbo said. "I'll take care of the gear while you drive over to your uncle's house and pick up the things he needs."

Brad opened the front door of his uncle's house, carrying the list of clothes and other things his uncle requested in his hand. His first stop was the kitchen, where he found a box of plastic garbage bags he could use to hold the items he hoped to find. He unrolled two, stuffed one in his back pocket and attempted to open one on his way his uncle's bedroom. *We can put a man on the moon*, he thought, *but we can't make rolls of plastic bags that open easily.*

He went to the dresser and looked in the drawers. He found that each drawer contained different articles of clothing, and was impressed at how organized his uncle was. From top to bottom, they appeared to be arranged in the order in which he would put them on.

Brad never pictured his uncle as anal-retentive. There were probably a lot of things about him he didn't know, Brad thought, as he opened the sliding closet doors to find suits, sport jackets, pants, shirts, belts and ties arranged neatly in their own areas on the clothes rack. Twenty or more pairs of shoes rested neatly on a shoe rack according to color. Had it been any other way, Brad wouldn't have given it another thought, but his uncle's almost obsessive-compulsive organization of his clothing was like a red flag in front of Brad's eyes. It was like the other times, a feeling of something that just didn't fit. Maybe he was being paranoid.

Brad gathered the things on the list, but his gaze kept going back to the shoes. He tried to shake it off, but couldn't. Finally, he pulled over a chair from the corner and sat down so he could view the part of the room that disturbed him. He looked from dresser to closet and back again, asking himself what was wrong with the picture. Running a successful business requires organization, so why did this organization disturb him? What was wrong with owning twenty pairs of shoes? Some people had hundreds of neckties.

Brad, of course, had only one. He tried to remember how many pairs of shoes his father had owned. Not nearly twenty. He remembered how particular his father had been about keeping his shoes shined. "If the army taught me anything, it was how to shine my shoes," he would say.

Brad couldn't recall if his uncle had been in the service. Then it hit him: it was the shine! One of the pairs of shoes among the twenty-odd others, looked dirty. Brad jumped to his feet, and picked one of the scuffed shoes from the rack. He turned it over in his hands, observing the small amount of mud still clinging to the inner portion of the heel. The heel, he was quite certain, was the same brand as the muddy print he found on the boat dock after the fire.

Some detective I am, he thought. I managed to find a shoe print at my uncle's factory that belongs to my uncle! Still, for reasons he could not explain, a chill ran down his spine.

He put all of the things he collected into the bag and, hoisting it over his shoulder like Santa Claus, walked out of the house.

Arriving at the garage, Brad found Jimbo and his uncle sitting in the small inner office, sharing a six-pack. He set the bag in the corner, brushed the dust from a chair, straddled it and reached for one of the sweating bottles. "Don't mind if I do," he said, twisting the cap off and taking a long drink.

George Allen broke the silence. "Jimbo told me how much you weighed in." He couldn't hide his enthusiasm, but Brad thought he detected a hint of envy in his tone. Brad didn't dwell on it. After all, he thought, it was his uncle who invited him to be his fishing partner in the tournament. It was only natural he would feel cheated by the series of events that had transpired.

Brad tried to make his uncle feel more a part of the team. "Have you got any suggestions for tomorrow's strategy?" he asked. That seemed to ease some of the tension Brad felt, whether real or imagined. His uncle and Jimbo immediately engaged in a running discussion, covering everything from wind direction to the weather report, boat position to bait selection, and lure color to water color. But Brad could not keep his mind on the conversation. He kept thinking about the final weigh-in, the Styrofoam cooler filled with bundles of money, and curiously enough, the glistening, sweaty body of the sheriff.

10

Brad watched as his uncle's head rose out of the water, sputtering and gasping for breath. In slow motion he cast toward him, hearing the accentuated buzz of the reel as the line flew toward it's target. Again and again, he repeated his cast. The buzzing seemed to get louder and louder, but still he could not reach his uncle. With a look of horror on his face, George Allen disappeared beneath the surface. Brad threw and retrieved and turned the reel's handle faster and faster. The buzzing increased in volume until his ears were ringing with pain.

Brad awoke soaked in perspiration. He reached over to stop the buzzing of the alarm clock. He shook himself to clear the cobwebs of sleep from his mind and return his breathing to normal. Rarely did a dream affect him so deeply. It took several minutes for him to remember where he was and why the alarm had dragged him back to reality.

He recalled leaving his uncle and Jimbo locked in heated conversation, promising to return in time for their run to the marina. He hurriedly performed his morning ritual. The dream already forgotten, his thoughts focused on the day's activities, clearing his mind of everything not pertaining to fishing. After all, he thought, concentration and confidence were as important to winning as proper equipment.

Brad thought it seemed cooler as he got into the pickup truck and started down the road to his uncle's garage. A mist hugged the surface of the road like a layer of smoke below the headlight beams. As he turned into the access road, he could hear the sputter and pop of the highly modified engine. Seeing Jimbo walking from the dock, Brad slowed to a halt.

Jimbo approached the truck window and said, "Hurry up and park that thing! We've got to leave now! A heavy fog is forming on the water. We'll be lucky to find the marina unless we hurry!"

Jimbo turned and hurried back to the boat. Brad quickly parked the car, and followed at a run. Brad cast off the lines, acknowledging the fact by gently nudging Jimbo's shoulder. He fastened his vest and settled himself in the passenger seat. Jimbo edged the boat from the dock, picking up speed as he reached the middle of the channel.

The sky was clear. The moonlight caused the top of the rapidly forming fog to glow with an eerie luminescence. The running lights were a diffused blob. Only the amber trace of the depth sounder was clearly defined. Brad was thankful Jimbo was at the helm, as he had already become disoriented by the fog. Soon, Brad could barely see the trolling motor on the bow of the boat. Only when a large marker buoy appeared, flew down the side and disappeared at the stern, was he assured they were still in the boat lane.

Jimbo's eyes were everywhere. But mostly he watched the G.P.S. and the compass, slowing only to make a sharp turn. Then, backing off on the throttle to no-wake speed, Jimbo idled into what Brad hoped was the marina's cove.

Brad's heart resumed its normal pace when he heard the rumble of other outboards above the purr of their engine. Soon, he saw the faint red and green glow of running lights, the fog all but obscuring the white of the anchor lights.

"No need to rush now," Jimbo commented. "They'll delay the start until the fog lifts."

And as if on cue, a voice pierced the fog, announcing, "For the safety of the tournament participants, the first flight will be delayed until such time as the judges deem it safe to proceed."

Jimbo strode to the bow, lowered the trolling motor and headed for the dock to check in and have the live well inspected. Other bass boats emerged from the fog like shimmering ghosts, then disappeared quickly as they slid past. The dock lights formed into solid objects, people taking shape as they moved slowly forward.

The inspection finished, Jimbo steered them into a vacant slip. "We might as well go in and get a hot cup of coffee and something to eat. We should have plenty of time before this fog begins to lift."

An hour after first light, a strong northeasterly wind combined with clear skies to burn off the fog. Unfortunately, the bluebird sky and persistent wind made the fishing as bad, or even worse, than yesterday. Nevertheless, Brad and Jimbo now in the third flight, the result of flip-flopping the order, had every assurance of doing well.

For the better part of two hours they fought the wind in open water, trying to fish deep main and secondary lake points, but with no results. Finally, in frustration, Jimbo declared, "I don't know about you son, but I'm getting tired of wasting the trolling motor batteries and watching the line blow back in my face. I'm for finding a likely-looking lee shore, and hope we hit some bass on the head."

Brad agreed, pointing out that yesterday had actually been more a matter of luck, and perhaps their luck would hold today. They both agreed that in spite of knowing what bass should do under any condition, there are times when they just can't be caught.

Under the awful conditions, Brad decided to stick with his confidence lure, the black rattle jig and black plastic pig. On the other hand, Jimbo tried a variety of lures and combinations. At the end of their allotted time, Brad caught and boated four keepers. Not getting so much as a strike, Jimbo grudgingly admitted, "You just plain outfished me, son!"

They left plenty of time for the trip in. The wind continued to blow with increasing force from the northeast. The white-tipped rollers, driven the length of the lake, made it a slow ride to the marina. The boat hurdled from crest to crest, its speed timed perfectly to the frequency of the waves. This was, in no little part due to the superb handling of the craft and Jimbo's seamanship. Brad marveled at the relatively smooth ride, shaken only when an occasional rogue wave mistimed their speed or drove the bow higher, causing it to thunder down onto the next one.

Ultimately, they reached the point where they sheared off to starboard for the final run to the marina. Jimbo skillfully adjusted the speed of the boat, so that their forward momentum equaled the speed of the waves. This enabled them to stay in the trough of one wave until they cleared the point of land that sheltered them from the main lake turbulence. They were once again in calm water, broken only by the occasional passage of another returning fisherman.

At the weigh-in, Jimbo fairly beamed with pride as the scale displayed their day's catch at nine and one-half pounds, making their two-day total twenty-eight pounds, twelve ounces. They won handily, and for the second time in almost as many days, Brad found himself having to make a speech in front of a throng of excited fishermen and spectators. Jimbo and he had discussed the possibility of winning the tournament, and had agreed what they would do.

Calling the crowd to attention, Reed Hadley emotionlessly handed the microphone to Brad.

"First of all, I would just like to say that I hope none of you have a problem with the fact that I'm George Allen's nephew and my partner, Jimbo, is, or was, the foreman at the boat factory."

A faint grumble traveled through the crowd as Brad continued, "I am as surprised as any of you. However, I can't say that Jimbo and I didn't discuss the possibility of winning. We agreed that any and all of our winnings, including the proceeds from the sale of the bass boat, would be divided among the employees to help tide you over until such time as the factory is rebuilt, or you find other jobs."

Anything else he might have felt like saying would have been drowned out by the wild cheering. He jumped down off the stage and was immediately mobbed by people shaking his hand and patting him on the back. Brad looked up and into Jimbo's face, its craggy lines broken by a huge smile. His outstretched hand offered Brad a dripping bottle of beer. At that moment, it was the greatest reward he could have hoped for.

Brad and Jimbo spent the rest of the afternoon milling about, retelling the details of each fish caught, embellishing each repetition as only a dedicated fisherman could. But as the crowd dwindled, Brad's mind began to drift to the white Styrofoam cooler, the dumpster and the stage. He hoped the sheriff remembered to put it in the seat of his uncle's pickup truck, as Jimbo had offered to drive the boat back and return with the truck and cooler. Meanwhile, Brad made as if the beer was going to his head, and sat on the steps of the stage. He looked up glassily, pretending to concentrate on his name, written in large letters on the leader board. His mind briefly considered his feelings for the sheriff. The fact that he thought of her as "the sheriff" rather than "Pat" said a lot.

Brad stared out at the lake. Beyond the entrance to the cove, he watched the waves churn. He could see the white horses smashing against the banks around the point. The lake was like a woman, he thought. Sometimes it was calm and sometimes, like today, it was raging. What made him wary of Pat was the same thing that made him wary of rough water: he didn't understand it and he couldn't control it. Unable to control his racing thoughts, he began to wish he had drunk more beer.

The sun was just beginning to touch the surface of the water. The wind was dying, and the waves were starting to lie down. The last of the boats had been pulled from the water, the fish had been released, the last of the beer had been consumed and the last fishing story had been retold. When Brad looked around, he found himself quite alone.

Jimbo sat in the truck, parked near a sign declaring "Car and Trailer Parking Only." He was in full view of the boat ramp, but only part of the platform was visible beyond the corner of the building. He looked all around. The parking lot appeared empty. On the seat next to him sat the white Styrofoam cooler. He had taken the opportunity to peer inside, just to make sure the money was indeed in there.

Brad crossed the parking lot in front of the ship's store and restaurant. He saw the lone pickup parked in the ramp area lot, and recognized Jimbo seated behind the wheel. Removing the cooler from the passenger seat and nodding to Jimbo, Brad retraced his steps to the platform, and with a final look around, placed it under the side nearest the dumpster. As arranged, Jimbo drove to the corner of the building and Brad got in. Jimbo made a big show of turning around and starting for the exit. But as they passed the rear of the building, Brad dove out of the truck and ran along its back side. Jimbo continued out of the parking lot, turned onto the highway, and drove off.

During the fog delay that morning, Brad had found a spot where he was totally concealed behind a wooden privacy fence. It was built to protect the building's refrigeration units. He crouched next to a large condensing unit. The heat from the condensing fan and the vibration of the compressor caused the beads of perspiration forming on his forehead to drip into his eyes. He tried to ignore the sting while staring through the small gap between the boards. His view was right at the edge of the stage. Squinting and moving his head, he could see part of the dumpster and the white cooler. He shifted his weight, trying to ease the cramping in his back and legs, and finally changing position. The gravel fill, scattered around to discourage weed growth, dug into his knees. He read the name and serial numbers on the machine in an attempt to take his mind off the pain. It wasn't working.

Just as he was about to switch to a seated position, a shadow flashed in front of his field of vision. He nearly stopped breathing, not only to be sure he made no noise, but to steady himself. He saw part of a body bend down and pick up the Styrofoam cooler. He hadn't heard a car pull up, so he assumed the person would have to go back along the fence, at the end of which he would be waiting. Then he would see.

Brad crept steadily along behind the fence, doing a kind of duck walk. Reaching the end, he saw the white cooler go past. In one movement, he stepped out, grabbing the person's right arm and, putting his own left around the person's throat, pulled back. The cooler spilled to the ground while a yelp of pain and surprise escaped from the slightly built individual. The arm Brad had in his grip felt soft and not heavily muscled, almost like a girl's arm. And the yell had a feminine sound, too.

"Say, what's this all about?" he asked, spinning the person around. His mouth fell open. He was frozen with confusion as he looked down into the face of Pat.

And that's when the lights went out.

Jimbo sat in his truck in the driveway of the mobile home park, next door to the marina. He had a view of the marina and its parking lot. He and Brad had arranged to meet after Brad found out who picked up the money. Brad Allen had no desire to be a dead hero. He would try to identify the person, or perhaps get a good description and possibly a license plate number. But the sheriff had told him that under no circumstances was he to try to apprehend the person. The one thing they had going for them was that no one else knew George Allen was alive and well, and free. They didn't have to worry that a mistake could cost his life.

Jimbo was a singularly simple man. Not that he wasn't intelligent, for he was. Not that he wasn't compassionate and caring, he was all that and more. It was just that he wasn't complex. He never cared to play any games. If he felt like commenting about himself, he would say, "What you see is what you get!"

Jimbo was also fiercely loyal to George Allen. And for reasons he didn't fully understand, he felt even more so toward Brad Allen. He couldn't ever remember being so devoted to anyone since . . . but that was a long time ago. Being the simple man he was, his past was gone and forgotten, better not to dwell on it, and that was that.

The last of the red sun disappeared behind the horizon, leaving the darkening sky painted in a host of transparent colors. Jimbo watched the display in his rearview mirror, and was strangely moved. He looked around the parking lot as lengthening shadows began to obscure areas close to the building. He could easily imagine figures lurking in the darkened niches. He checked the time. Brad had been gone a long time.

A feeling of panic slowly crept over Jimbo. He often experienced this panic just before or after bad things had happened. He stepped carefully from the truck, walked around to the passenger side, reached into the glove compartment and brought out a flashlight. Keeping to the shadows, he worked his way from one tall pine tree to the next. The pine trees formed a natural fence line between the marina and the mobile home park. The lowest branches of the tall pines were at least ten feet above the ground, so they did not obstruct his view of the marina. As he crossed the median, with its sparse grass and spongy beds of pine needles, he thought he heard a car pull away. But a look toward the road showed no lights.

Jimbo visually scanned the parking lot as he jogged to the marina. Then, hugging the building, he inched his way around, using his flashlight to examine the dark recess formed by the building's uneven perimeter. He reached the corner nearest the dumpster and shined his light under the stage. Seeing no Styrofoam cooler, he continued to probe deeper beneath the platform, just in case something else, like a body, might be hidden there. The beam of his flashlight revealed assorted food and candy wrappers, several empty beer and soft drink cans and quite a few blackened soft plastic worms and lizards, looking dramatically realistic. But no bodies. Another search of the area netted him nothing. The marina itself was closed. All of the interior lights were turned off, with the exception of a neon beer sign in the window. A tall sodium vapor lamp cast its yellowish glow on the boat ramp, its blurry reflection rippling on the surface of the water.

Jimbo sat on the edge of the boat dock, and lowered his head into his hands. He had reached the limit of his investigative abilities. He needed a plan, or someone to come along and tell him what to do next. He thought of the sheriff. He could go see the sheriff, and she would know what he must do.

Driving toward town, Jimbo began to figure. Figuring didn't come easy to him. He liked to think long and slow, coming up with an idea only after much deliberation. This puzzle was missing too many pieces for him to reason it out. For instance, he had assumed the sheriff would be hiding nearby, along with several deputies, to capture the person who came for the cooler full of money. He probably misunderstood, he thought, as he found no sheriff, no money, and also no Brad. Another thing that was bothering him was the absence of George Allen when he went back to pick up the ransom money. He had been in too much of a hurry to look for a note or other clues to his whereabouts.

The first thing Brad noticed was the pain. It seemed to fill the large hollow object sitting on top of his neck. When he tried to lift one arm, the pain spilled out and down, causing incredible agony. A wave of nausea and dizziness passed over him when he tried to sit upright. Something warm and sticky trickled slowly down his neck. He was sure it was blood, but the thought of touching his head made him gag. He was also sure he couldn't see. Either the room was dark, or the hit on his head affected his eyesight. One thing was for sure, he had most of the symptoms of a concussion. Keeping his eyes open without the dizziness, eventually accustomed them to the dark. He looked slowly around the room, turning his whole body rather than his neck, for the pain was too great. He saw a sliver of light around what he took to be a door. Objects began to take shape. He recognized a cabinet or vanity, and next to that, a toilet. Although his head was still swimming, he decided he was in a restroom.

After what seemed like hours, Brad made an attempt to get over to the sink to put cold water on his aching head. As he drew a deep breath and summoned what was left of his strength, he heard voices. They appeared to come from the other side of the wall. He inched along the baseboard, trying to find a spot where the sounds were loudest. He leaned his head against the wall, pressing his ear as firmly as he dared without bringing back the pain. The voices stopped, as if they were listening, and then resumed. "As I was saying, Tucker didn't have to hit me at all, let alone so hard," the male voice complained.

A female voice replied, "I'd guess he did it partly to get even for that business at Dolly's place, and partly just to make it look like a kidnapping, in case anybody saw him. After all, it wouldn't have been much of a kidnapping if you just up and went away with him."

Brad's head was reeling. *It must be the concussion*, he thought. The voices sounded just like Uncle George and Pat.

"And another thing," the male voice continued, "How come y'all left me out there without food or drink so long?"

Brad was sure it was Pat who answered. "You're lucky you got back at all! Jimbo killed Tucker before he had a chance to tell anyone where he hid you. If it wasn't for the dumb luck of your meddling nephew, you'd still be there."

Besides the pain in his head, Brad felt as if he were just kicked in the stomach. He gagged, but nothing came of it. *This is all part of a bad dream*, he thought. But the pain and sickness were proof, if he needed more proof, that what was happening was very real. And, the thought came to him that his life was now in very real danger.

The idea of dying, especially at the hands of the two people whom he thought loved him, gave him a strength and determination he never felt before. He gathered himself together and took stock of his situation. Moving his hands over his body, he was encouraged to find he wasn't bound or otherwise restrained. It was only a matter of time before they quit talking about the past and started thinking of the future. Then, they would have to make sure he didn't meddle again.

Even though his vision was somewhat limited, Brad felt sure he was in the restroom off of the small office that separated the two bays of his uncle's garage.

He got slowly and carefully to his feet. Trying not to make any noise, and hoping the pain and dizziness did not return, Brad felt his way to the vanity. He put his right knee on one side of the sink and lifted the other, placing it on the left side of the sink. The effort brought the pain pounding like a hammer to his head. He felt the nausea begin to rise in his chest. Drawing upon his reserves, he refused to succumb to his weakness. This served to increase his resolve.

He straightened his body, walking his hands up the wall, over the medicine cabinet, to maintain his balance and feel what he was looking for. His fingers touched the metal channel of the grid which supported the drop ceiling. He felt the texture of the fiber material. With a gentle push upward, the room was illuminated by the light from the garage. He slid the ceiling tile sideways until he had enough room to pull his body up and over the back wall. As he suspected, the wall extended only inches above the ceiling and was tied into the roof trusses, enabling him to climb up and out of the bathroom. He stopped to replace the ceiling tile in its proper location. He hoped the acoustical material of the ceiling squares would absorb any noise he might have made.

The roof trusses were only on twenty-four-inch centers, making it difficult for Brad to cross from one to the next. The horizontal chord, upon which he had to stand, was only two-and-one-half inches wide, and his balance was already compromised by the blow he had received to his head. He had no accurate idea of what time of day it was, but enough light was coming in through roof and eave vents for him to see where he was going.

The area directly in front of him was the ceiling of the small office.

He could see the web of support wires which held the metal grid work and acoustical tiles. Evenly spaced among the ceiling tiles were four light fixtures. Kneeling uncomfortably on the nearest truss chord and looking through the louvered vents in the light housings, Brad could see who was in the office and hear what they were saying.

He repressed a moan as he saw his uncle and Pat below him. He no longer had any doubts of their complicity, although he wasn't quite sure of their motives. He listened to as much of their conversation as he dared, trying to gauge the moment when they would go to the restroom. Finding him gone, they were sure to begin a thorough search, which undoubtedly would reveal his whereabouts. He nearly panicked when a small brownish chameleon scampered across his hand, stopping just long enough to inflate its pouch several times, letting Brad know he was trespassing on its domain.

Not wanting to press his luck, Brad started looking for a way out. He hadn't the slightest idea of where he might go or what he would do if he got out. It was obvious he couldn't go to his uncle's house, or to Pat's for that matter. It was easy to think Jimbo was in it up to his neck with the others, but for some reason he found that thought harder to accept.

Brad had one other problem, he realized. The trusses he was now balancing on were nearly ten feet above a concrete floor, far higher than the distance which he thought he could jump with any hope of landing safely. A broken leg, or worse, would leave him no better off than he had been in the restroom. He gazed slowly around the garage, anxiously searching for anything that might serve as a ladder.

At the far end, fastened to one of the trusses, a chain hoist hung from a hook. If he could get to it, he might be able to climb down the chain, provided it wasn't too greasy. With luck, in a few minutes he was on the ground looking for a rag or something to wipe his dirty hands on. For a second, he considered going to the restroom to wash his hands with soap and water. "I must have been hit harder than I thought," he whispered to himself, suppressing a giggle.

There was a rear door a few feet away. The deadbolt lock, long unused, opened with moderate effort. Brad quietly shut the door, hoping once his captors realized he was missing, they would not immediately notice it was unlocked. Going left would take him around to the front of the garage and in full view of his uncle and Pat. Straight ahead were dense woods. He had no idea where they ended, but he was sure Pat or his uncle did. To the right was the lake. He knew he couldn't risk swimming, but if he could get to the boat dock, the keys might still be in the ignition of his uncle's boat. If not, he'd try drifting out of reach, then hot-wiring it. Once he got it started, he thought, nothing on the lake could catch him.

Brad looked along the side of the building. It was a solid wall, having no windows or doors. He felt fairly secure as long as he was in the shadows provided by the roof's overhang. The problem was, he would have about thirty yards to cross to the boat dock, with nothing to protect him from being seen. To make matters worse, he heard what sounded like highly agitated conversation and slamming of doors. He was sure they had discovered he was gone.

Brad summoned all of his reserve and sprinted for the dock. He dove the last few feet and rolled into the boat. Peering over the gunwale, he saw Pat aiming her service revolver at him, his uncle coming up behind her and his good friend Jimbo, at a full run, trying to cut him off on an angle. He felt the bullet pass next to his ear before he heard the report of the gun. He ducked his head and rolled slightly, spotting the keys dangling from the ignition. Reaching up, he turned the key, and the engine sputtered to life. He said aloud, "Thank goodness for electronic fuel injection," then turned to look again as two more shots rang out.

One must have over shot into the water, while the other raised a shower of splinters as it hit the dock. Brad was more concerned about Jimbo, but when he looked up, he saw the man running not for the boat, but straight at Pat. She must have seen him from the corner of her eye about the same time as Brad. She tried to turn, bringing the heavy gun to bear. In all of the excitement, the gun went off, a small cloud of dust kicked up where it hit the ground. She fired one last time before Jimbo hit her, his two hundred and sixty-plus pounds nailing her squarely in the throat. She'd be very lucky, Brad speculated, if she didn't have a broken neck to go with her broken ribs and a host of other body parts.

Brad's uncle stood as if frozen to the spot, only flinching as the shots rang out. His mouth was open, but no sounds came out. Jimbo didn't stop, but came running for the boat. Slowing only to untie the bow line, he jumped in, shouting, "Let's get the hell out of here!"

Brad had already untied the stern line. He contemplated attempting to tear the cleat from the dock using the power of the engine, but thought better of it. Jimbo sat on a rod locker with the line in his hand. Something was dripping from his fingers. At first, Brad thought it was water, but seeing Jimbo slump, he knew it was blood. He knew where the last bullet went. He also knew that Jimbo used himself as a target so the last two shots would not be aimed at him.

"Are you hurt bad, big guy?" Brad asked, slamming the throttle down. The boat leaped to life, launched itself from the dock.

I am now," Jimbo winced, trying to pick himself from the floor and crawl to a seat. "Next time you might warn me before you take off."

"Be serious," Brad admonished. "Do you need to go to a hospital?"

Jimbo replied, "Right now, getting safely out of gunshot range is worry enough for me. But if it will make you feel better, we'll head for the dam. The hospital is right across the road from the power plant. While I'm getting checked out, you'd best figure out what to do about this mess."

Not knowing if the sheriff was dead or alive, or what Brad's uncle would do now that at least part of his plan was uncovered, weighed heavily on both men's minds. At this very moment, there might be warrants for their arrest for murder or at the very least, assault and battery. Brad didn't think they'd take very kindly to assaulting or killing a sheriff, especially a female sheriff.

Running by water certainly wasn't the quickest way to get to the dam or the hospital. The hour-long run to the dam at cruising speed gave Brad time to enjoy the scenery, even though his mind was racing faster than the boat. He could see the topography change as they got closer. The sandy, tree-lined and grass covered banks gave way to rocky bluffs or outcroppings. Trees were seldom seen emerging from the water, which was clearer and much deeper. What coves he saw were V-shaped, with steep drop-offs and trees that appeared to grow right out of the stone walls. He also noticed the lack of boat lane markers and asked Jimbo why they ended so abruptly.

"All the water hereabouts is deep enough to run in. Why, there's probably a good twenty-five feet of water over the tops of the trees down there. Great striper fishing in the fall. Some of the local divers have told me of seeing fish down there bigger than a man."

Brad was about to comment when he saw Jimbo's head turn to look behind, then snap back. There was a strange look on his face.

"What is it?" Brad asked. He could see the effort Jimbo's mind was making.

Jimbo stuttered. "Th-the boat behind us. It's your uncle's old boat. Your uncle's driving it, coming right after us."

Brad tried to make his mind work. Ahead he could see the dam. It stretched across the entire width of the lake, both sides tapering off in huge mounds of rip-rap. At one end, a county park showed its steeply angled cul-de-sac, ending at twin boat ramps, each with its own floating dock. Jimbo pointed toward it, saying, "Head for the ramp. We'll tie up at the dock. The hospital is just over the hill and across the road."

"But what about Uncle George? He'll follow us," Brad replied.

"Let him!" was all that Jimbo said.

Brad backed off on the throttle, letting the forward momentum carry them into the no-wake zone. To his right he saw the large floating buoys with the Coast Guard "Danger" configurations and signs warning "Strong Currents, Keep Out!" They were strung out in a line across the water, well in back of the dam.

Brad watched as his uncle came flying by on plane. Apparently, he badly misjudged their pursuer's speed, and rather than risk swamping his craft, George had kept going straight. All the while, he was watching Brad and Jimbo. Suddenly, he turned his head, and seeing he had entered the dangerous area, tried desperately to reverse the throttle. He only succeeded in stalling the motor. Brad tried to yell to him, but he engaged himself in trying to restart the engine. Finally giving up his attempts, he ran to the bow and lowered the trolling motor.

Brad stared in horror as his uncle, leaning calmly against his butt seat like he was slowly working his way along a bank, tried to turn his boat out of the current. Either the current was too strong, or the old trolling motor just didn't have enough power. As Brad and Jimbo looked on, George Allen's boat was being drawn toward one of the giant iron clam-shell shutters that controlled the amount of water being sucked into the spillway. Once through the shutters, he would tumble a hundred feet down to the rocky turbulence of the river below.

George Allen looked at the steadily approaching dam. Then, he turned and looked toward Brad and Jimbo at the boat dock. A look of resignation came over his face. The boat had turned its stern onto the dam's face. George Allen's voice carried with an inhuman wail, "I'm sorrrrryyyy!" And like a door slamming shut, all was quiet. Boat, motor and George Allen disappeared.

Brad and Jimbo ran as fast as they could up the access road to the highway, and followed it to where it crossed the dam. They stood looking down into the mist above the roaring tail race waters, their breath coming in great gasps.

When his breathing finally returned to normal, Jimbo said, shaking his massive head, "Nobody could survive a drop like that. If the fall didn't kill him, the current and the rocks surely would. The water will hold him down and tumble his body against the rocks until there's nothing left of him."

Much later, Brad and Jimbo found themselves in the courthouse, in the office of the County Prosecutor, County Coroner and Building Inspector. Sitting behind a well-worn oak desk was a barrel of a man, his sweat-stained shirt open at the collar, his knotted necktie loosely askew. His threadbare sport jacket appeared to be several sizes too large. The plastic plate in front of the five-year-old desk calendar said *John Amos*. Brad couldn't help but wonder which one of the three titles he held. For all he knew, John Amos might be all three.

A booming voice announced, "You boys are mighty lucky. We got a complete confession from the sheriff before she died. If it hadn't been for that, both of you'd be in jail right now. You could have been charged with two counts of murder, kidnapping, conspiracy, fraud and about two dozen other things I can't pronounce. But just for the record, I'd like to hear what happened in your own words."

Brad related his experiences over the past week. Jimbo, having taken part in a good portion of it, merely nodded his head, unable to add anything substantial until the end. He then told about Brad failing to return after leaving the cooler full of money, going to the sheriffs office and not finding her there, then returning to the garage to find Pat shooting at Brad with George standing and watching.

"What I still don't understand," Brad asked, "is what part I was supposed to play in all of this."

The big man behind the desk drew himself up as if with a great effort, sighed and began to speak. "As near as we can figure, not only was your uncle a lousy businessman, he wasn't a very lucky gambler. He got himself into trouble with the syndicate by trying to cover his gambling losses with the boat business. The mob bosses checked it out, and found not only did he overstate his boat sales, but he didn't even own the property. You see, they had been slowly buying up land around the cove with the idea of building a casino and hotel complex. All strictly legal. They laundered dirty money by buying the land through a front corporation. They called it the Harley Deer Corporation.

"Our office was first notified of their part in it by a local banker, Reed Hadley. He complained that people would think he owned the corporation because of the similarity between his name spelled backwards or upside down or something, and the syndicate's name. Anyhow, it seems your uncle set up some schemes to make it look like someone was trying to kill him. And then you were to be killed by mistake, leaving him as the last surviving heir and owner of the property."

"But what did the sheriff have to do with it?" Brad asked, trying to force his mind to accept what he was being told.

Resuming his narrative, Amos said, "She actually got involved quite by mistake. While investigating the so-called accidents your uncle reported, she became suspicious. When she confronted him, he broke down and told her the whole scenario. By this time, your uncle had grown quite fond of you. It turns out you're not the pampered, snot-nosed, professional student he thought you were.

"That's when they came up with the plan to fake his kidnapping. You did exactly as they hoped. This way they could get the money and after ten days, the land would belong to the bank when you defaulted on the loan. You go home, your uncle turns up, and later on, he or the corporation would have bought the land from the bank. The sheriff sells her piece for top dollar and everybody's happy.

"But, as luck would have it, Jimbo killed Tucker Jones and the two of you accidentally stumble across your uncle. This drives the sheriff up a wall. Your uncle wants to call the whole thing off, but Pat figures they can still make it work. Bingo! You're the fly in the ointment again. If it wasn't for Jimbo here, you'd be pushin' up daisies right now. You're either the luckiest or the unluckiest s.o.b. I've ever met in my life. I can't decide which."

The lengthy dissertation seemed to wear the man out. He slumped back into his wooden swivel rocker and, clasping his hands across the vast expanse of his midsection, closed his eyes as if to end his part in the interview.

Epilogue

It was typical that the next week brought mild, stable weather. The kind that's usually associated with "Boy, right after you left, the fish really turned on!" Brad stayed at Jimbo's house while legal matters were settled. As it turned out, the late George Allen had a will. He left everything to his brother. Being the only living heir, what was left after all claims were satisfied went straight to Brad. It wasn't a fortune, but with an unpretentious lifestyle, Brad was free to pursue his dream of tournament fishing.

Brad felt a sudden twinge of regret. He sped his retrieve as though to shake off the memories that assailed him. He didn't like to think about his all-too-recent losses. First his parents, then his uncle and Pat. Even though the inquest had honorably acquitted Jimbo and him, strangely enough, the passing days made his feelings about the incidents sharper instead of duller.

He felt a sort of sympathy for his uncle, and pity for Pat. A poor substitute for love, and yet the memory of their brief affair hurt intensely. Recent events kept coming to life again in his mind. The horrible realization of how he was badly used was more disturbing than physical reminders. Jimbo leaned against his butt seat on the rear casting deck, his arm still in a sling from the bullet wound he had received while trying to protect Brad. He was still able to cast, although not quite achieving his usual distance. Brad gazed at him. He was as loyal and understanding as any wife or mother. He understood his moods, and yet he was undemanding. Brad's thoughts were instantly thrust into the background as Jimbo yelled, "Set the hook!"

The cobwebs cleared as Brad swept his rod sideways, feeling the resistance as the rod tip jigged wildly. After a brief struggle, he gently lipped a seven-pound-plus bass. "That's what we're here for," he casually remarked, his mind no longer wrapped up in the past.

His heart was still pounding with excitement. He stared along the shore at the beauty of the trees and flowers. He could hear the songs of the birds and the sounds of countless creatures going about their daily lives. He looked at the huge grin that erased the years from Jimbo's face. His mind was at rest. His thoughts were focused. He was ready to make his next cast.